Swap'd

Swap'd

Tamara Ireland Stone

DISNEY · HYPERION
Los Angeles   New York

First Edition, February 2019
10 9 8 7 6 5 4 3 2 1
FAC-020093-18355
Printed in the United States of America

This book is set in Janson MT Pro, Andale Mono MT Pro,
Adderville ITC/Monotype; KG Happy/Fontspring
Designed by Phil Caminiti, Andrew Brozyna, and Mary Claire Cruz
Photographs and art by Andrew Brozyna • Alias Ching/Shutterstock •
PureSolution/Shutterstock • CREATISTA/Shutterstock • Raisa Kanareva/
Shutterstock • Rawpixel.com/Shutterstock • dourleak/Shutterstock • phloxii/
Shutterstock • Andrej Sevkovskij/Shutterstock • ShotPrime Studio/Shutterstock
• Jennie Book/Shutterstock • Lunatictm/Shutterstock • Zilu8/Shutterstock
• Vladimir Sukhachev/Shutterstock • Fitria Ramli /Shutterstock

Library of Congress Cataloging-in-Publication Data
Names: Stone, Tamara Ireland, author.
Title: Swap'd / Tamara Ireland Stone.
Other titles: Swapped
Description: First edition. • Los Angeles ; New York : Disney•Hyperion, 2019. •
Series: [Click'd ; 2] • Summary: "After building one wildly popular app, Allie Navarro
is ready for her next coding challenge—earning enough money for a trip to
Game On Con with her friend, Courtney"— Provided by publisher.
Identifiers: LCCN 2018042030 (print) • LCCN 2018048951 (ebook) •
ISBN 9781484798492 (e-book) • ISBN 9781484786963 (hardcover) •
ISBN 9781484798652 (pbk.)
Subjects: • CYAC: Application software—Fiction. • Computer games—Fiction. •
Computer programming—Fiction. • Friendship—Fiction. • Moneymaking projects—
Fiction. • Middle schools—Fiction. • Schools—Fiction.
Classification: LCC PZ7.S8814 (ebook) • LCC PZ7.S8814 Sw 2019 (print) •
DDC [Fic]—dc23
LC record available at https://lccn.loc.gov/2018042030

Reinforced binding

Visit www.DisneyBooks.com

SUSTAINABLE FORESTRY INITIATIVE   Certified Sourcing
www.sfiprogram.org
SFI-00993

THIS LABEL APPLIES TO TEXT STOCK

Aidan, this one's for you

sunday

one

**Attention, teen coders!
Want to spend your summer at Spyglass Games?**

We're looking for students in grades 6–12 to help create the company's first teen hackathon!

Hackathons are "hacking marathons" that pit team against team in a weekend-long, beat-the-clock coding competition. Work together to create a game, mobile app, or even a robot—in just two days, totally from scratch—and you could win big cash (and big-time bragging rights)!

But first, we need your help creating the perfect summer program. As part of our exclusive development team, you'll take part in your choice of three hackathon weekends, all held on our beautiful San Francisco campus, where you'll share ideas and feedback that will help shape the Spyglass Teen Hackathon for years to come. Come take part in this truly unique, once-in-a-lifetime opportunity! Applicants must have at least two years of coding experience and demonstrate the ability to work quickly and collaboratively. Space is extremely limited. Good luck!

Allie leaned back against her headboard and adjusted the laptop in front of her. She scanned her application one more time to be sure she hadn't missed anything.

Current Grade: 7
Coding Experience: 3 years, Games for Good Finalist
Most Recent Project (include link to demo): Click'd

Click'd. She loved her game, but she wished she had something more recent to share with the selection committee. Something they hadn't already seen. Something they hadn't already seen bomb so spectacularly.

She scrolled down to her essay and read it out loud. It sounded pretty good.

"What do you think, Bo?" Her dog opened one eye when he heard his name, but then closed it again. He snuggled in closer to her hip and tipped his head back so Allie could rub that spot under his chin.

"You're right. I should just send it."

The application wasn't due until the end of the month, but she'd been working on it for weeks. Her mom and dad had both read her essay countless times, and so had her computer science teacher, Ms. Slade. There was no reason to wait. Nothing was going to change before it was due anyway.

She listened to the rain plinking against her bedroom window while her finger hovered over the submit button.

She was about to click it, when her phone chirped. Bo jumped so high, his body practically left the bed.

She laughed as she reached for the phone and read the text.

Courtney

Good day/bad day?

Allie and Courtney usually did good day/bad day right before they fell asleep at night, just like they used to when they were roommates at CodeGirls Camp the previous summer. But they'd been missing each other more than usual lately, and they seemed to be starting the routine earlier.

Allie

Scored a goal in soccer game today
Went to a movie with my friends
Spyglass sent me passes to Game On

She was waiting for Courtney to respond when the familiar FaceTime ring echoed in the room.

"You're going to Game On Con?" Courtney stared at Allie wide-eyed. Her hair was piled on top of her head in a messy bun, and she was wearing her favorite SUNDAY FUNDAY T-shirt.

Allie sat up straighter. "Um . . . Yeah."

"Game On Con. *The* Game On Con?"

"I'm pretty sure there's only one of them." Spyglass Games held it every January and people came from all over the world to attend, making downtown San Francisco heaven-on-earth for the gaming community. "Because of Click'd, I get to go for free and check out all the new games and stuff."

Allie wasn't about to tell her about the personal meet-and-greet with the CEO, Naomi Ryan. Or how she'd planned to use that time to try to land a spot in the summer hackathon program. Courtney couldn't know about Hackathon. Not yet.

"Nathan's going, too," she said.

Nathan got an even sweeter deal than Allie had. He'd been invited to be onstage during Naomi Ryan's keynote and attend some swanky dinner thing with the development team.

"But you don't even play video games!"

"Sure I do."

Courtney let out a huff. "Name one game you play."

Allie thought about it. She had an old Nintendo DS around her room somewhere, but she hadn't turned it on in years. Besides, she knew that wouldn't count. Courtney was talking about real games, like the ones she played every day after school with her online friends.

Courtney didn't give Allie time to reply. "You're so

lucky. Stuff like this happens right in your *backyard*, all the time. Nothing cool ever happens in Phoenix."

"You have more sun," Allie tried.

"Ha! You can have it. I mean, come on . . . it's January. Right now, it's snowing in half the country, but it's seventy-five degrees here. *Seventy-five degrees*, Allie. That's just not natural!"

Courtney had one of those loud, contagious laughs. Hearing her now reminded Allie of those days in the computer lab over the summer. Courtney's giggle would turn into a full-on belly laugh, and that would make Allie laugh, and then Maya would hear them, and she'd start laughing. That would trigger Kaiya and Li at the next station, and soon everyone in the Fishbowl would be wiping their eyes and trying to catch their breaths, and no one but Courtney and Allie would even know what was so funny in the first place.

"Well, it's been raining for four days straight here in San Francisco," Allie said. "So if you need a break from all that horrible sunshine, you can always come here."

Courtney flopped back onto her bed and lifted the phone high in the air. "Don't tempt me. I'd be there in a heartbeat. And I'll gladly take one of those Game On tickets off your hands."

And then they both got quiet. Courtney stared up at Allie's face on her screen. Allie stared back at Courtney.

"Actually . . ." Allie said slowly, watching the idea start

coming to life in her mind. "They *did* tell me to give my extra pass to a friend."

Courtney rested her hand on her chest. "Last time I checked, *I* was your friend."

"You are most *definitely* my friend." Allie threw her feet to the floor and tapped her toes on her carpet. "Come visit me for the weekend!"

"Really?"

"Sure! We'll go to Game On and then I can spend the rest of the weekend showing you San Francisco! We'll walk across the Golden Gate Bridge, and visit Alcatraz, and go to the top of Coit Tower. We'll do all the things we couldn't do when you were here for camp last summer."

Allie's parents would be so excited. They loved acting like tourists in their own city.

"We'll get hot chocolate at my favorite place in North Beach," Allie continued. "And you can meet Maddie, Emma, and Zoe—they are *so* tired of hearing me talk about you—and you can finally meet Nathan!"

Courtney was on her feet now. She must have been dancing around her room because all Allie could see were bookshelves, her desk, her bed, and her window, all blurring by.

"Allie!" Courtney stopped moving. "That's only two weeks away!"

"Well, today is Sunday, and you'd have to get here on a Friday, so technically it's only twelve days from now."

"Twelve days!" Courtney yelled.

"Twelve sleeps!" Allie added.

Allie pictured Courtney walking through the airport security gates, beaming at her from the top of the escalator. She couldn't wait to throw her arms around Courtney's neck and pull her into the tightest hug she'd ever given her.

"Will your parents say yes?" Courtney asked.

"Sure! I mean, I think so! The conference is free, and you're only one state away . . . the flight couldn't be *that* expensive. And they know how much I miss you!" Allie was talking so fast she had to stop to catch her breath. "Your parents will say yes, too, right?"

"Of course they will!"

Allie ran to her desk and sat down in her chair. She propped the phone up next to her keyboard and opened a browser to one of the online ticketing services. She entered the data into the empty fields:

From: Phoenix

To: San Francisco

Allie hit ENTER. The icon spun in place as the system told her it was searching for the lowest price. Courtney flopped down in her denim beanbag chair, chewing nervously on her fingernail while she waited. Times and flight numbers began filling the screen. There was a celebratory sound as the "fabulous fare" landed at the top.

Allie gulped. She stared in disbelief for a long moment. And then she angled her phone so Courtney could see the screen.

"Four *hundred* dollars! Seriously?"

"Seriously," Allie said.

"How could it be four hundred dollars? It's, like, a two-hour flight. Search it again."

Allie searched it again. Same spinning icon. Same "fabulous fare." Same lump in her throat.

They'd been so excited about it being less than two weeks away, but that was the problem. Allie searched dates further into the future, and sure enough, those tickets were half the price.

"It's too soon." Allie fell back in her chair, feeling totally deflated.

"Do you have any money?" Courtney asked.

Allie shook her head. "None. I spent it all on Christmas presents."

"Same here. I found five bucks in my backpack the other day, but that's all I've got."

"Maybe our parents will split it?"

Courtney laughed again, but this time, there was nothing funny or contagious about it. "Yeah, right."

"It can't hurt to ask," Allie said. "I'll tell them I'll do extra jobs. I'll mow the lawn and give Bo a bath."

"I'll wash the car and babysit my little brother for free," Courtney said.

"They have to say yes."

Courtney got serious again. "I have to go to Game On, Allie. I need to get out of here. I need rain, and you, and thousands of nerdy gamers like me, and—"

"Allie! Dinner!" her mom called from the bottom of the stairs.

Bo knew that word. He ran straight for her bedroom door and sat there, tail wagging, waiting for Allie to open it so he could follow the smells that led to the kitchen.

"Wish me luck." Allie gave the phone screen a fist bump.

"Luck," Courtney said, bumping her back.

two

"There you are." Allie's dad wiped his hands on a kitchen towel. "I thought I was going to have to stand outside your bedroom door holding this pizza box to coax you out."

Allie closed her eyes, took a big inhale. "You ordered pizza?" They always had pizza on Fridays, but on Sundays, her parents usually cooked dinner together.

"We decided we were too cold and hungry to cook." Her mom folded her arms across her chest and shivered. Her hair was still wet from sitting in the rain during Allie's soccer game that afternoon. "We spent the day getting drenched in the stands. We figured we all deserved pizza."

"And no dishes," her dad added as he filled three glasses with water and set them on the table.

Allie could practically taste the cheese melting in her mouth. It was the perfect addition to the fire going in the living room and the sound of the raindrops against the kitchen windows. She hadn't realized how hungry she was, but now she reached for a slice and took a huge bite.

"What are you working on up there?" her dad asked. "Big test tomorrow?"

Allie shook her head. "No. I'm done with homework. I was talking with Courtney."

"Of course," her mom said. "How often do you two talk each day?"

"I don't know. A bunch. I don't really keep count."

They texted all the time and they FaceTimed each other even more. Courtney had volleyball practice after school, but she always called Allie the second she got home. They'd chat while they were doing homework, and sometimes, if they weren't too tired, right after Allie got home from soccer practice. And that didn't even include their good day/bad day text exchanges, which they never, ever missed, even if they were exhausted. They were on a 162-day streak.

"We were just talking about how much we miss each other," Allie tried to keep her voice light and casual. "And you know, she's not that far away. We were thinking maybe she could come visit?"

"Of course. We'd love that," her mom said.

"She's welcome any time," her dad added. "Maybe she could come for spring break?"

"Actually . . ." Allie rested her elbows on the table. "We were thinking she could come for Game On?"

Her mom took a bite of pizza. Her dad popped a forkful of salad into his mouth. It was silent while they chewed.

"That's only two weeks away," her mom finally said as she reached for her water glass.

"I know, but Courtney has always wanted to go to Game On, and I have two free tickets, and of all my friends, she'd love it most, and she's never been to San Francisco. She was here for CodeGirls camp last summer, but we spent the whole time on the Fuller University campus, so that doesn't really count. We were miles away from the best stuff. She never even saw the ocean. Or Alcatraz. Or the Golden Gate Bridge." Allie knew she was rambling. She stopped to take a breath. And a bite. Because the pizza was just sitting there under her nose, and it smelled delicious, and her stomach was grumbling.

"You've already looked into flights, haven't you?" her mom asked.

Allie nodded.

"How much is the ticket?"

"Four hundred dollars," she said quietly.

Her parent's eyebrows shot up in unison.

"Four hundred dollars?" her dad repeated.

"From Phoenix?" her mom asked.

"That's ridiculous," her dad said.

"Well, last-minute fares are always overpriced. Remember that trip to Denver I had to take last month?" Her mom let out a huff. "Outrageous."

Allie's dad looked at her. "That's out of the question."

Her mom took another bite. "Clearly."

And then it got quiet again.

Allie approached with caution. "What if you split the cost with her parents?"

Her mom started to talk, and Allie could tell she was going to say no, so she didn't give her a chance. "I'll do extra chores. You don't have to give me my allowance for a month. I'll do anything!"

"You make five dollars a week, Allie. Last time I checked, that adds up to twenty dollars a month."

"Fine, you can keep my allowance for the rest of the school year! I don't need anything."

Her parents exchanged a glance.

"Why is this suddenly so important to you?" her mom asked.

Allie didn't know how to explain it. It wasn't as if Courtney was a better friend than Emma, Maddie, and Zoe, but it was different. Courtney understood Allie in a way no one else did. It wasn't just that they both loved coding; it was more than that.

It was the way they worked together in the lab all summer, late into the night, sharing sodas and gummy worms, making up inside jokes, cracking up at everything and nothing at all. And it was the way they cheered each other

15

on when the program got tough, when they wanted to give up, when one of them didn't think she could take the pressure any more, and the other one convinced her she was stronger, tougher, and smarter than she thought she was. Neither one ever had to ask for the other's help. It was like they each had a sixth sense. And, as silly as it may have seemed to anyone else, it was the way they landed on each other's Click'd leaderboard in that number one spot, out of all twenty CodeGirls. That meant something neither one of them could explain. They started out strangers, but after everything they'd been through, it was as if Click'd knew they were meant to be friends all along.

But none of that really answered her mom's question about why it was *suddenly* so important. That was something else entirely.

"What if I get picked for Hackathon?" Allie asked. "Then I won't be going to CodeGirls Camp with Courtney this summer. If she comes to Game On, at least I can tell her in person that I applied."

Allie thought about the application, complete and just waiting to be submitted. It was a long shot; Spyglass was only taking forty kids—ten middle schoolers and thirty high school students—and the company was selecting them from all over the state.

The chances of her going were slim to none. Her chances were even worse since she hadn't developed anything since Click'd. And her chances were *worser than worse* since the Spyglass CEO, Naomi Ryan, was personally involved in the internship selection process, and she only knew Allie one way: the kid who bombed at the Games for Good competition four months earlier.

"Look," her mom said, snapping Allie back to reality. "We know how much you and Courtney miss each other. And we'd love to have her come visit—we really would—but let's do it in a month or so. You save your money, let her save her portion, and buy a ticket in advance. Then I bet round-trip will cost closer to two hundred bucks."

"Maybe even one-fifty," her dad added.

"That's nothing."

"You two can totally save that."

They nodded at each other. Then looked back at Allie again.

"We'll make you a deal," her mom said. "You two pay for her plane ticket and we'll cover everything while she's here. Museums, Alcatraz, the works. We'll take her anywhere she wants to go. All you have to do is cover the flight."

"And it will be warmer," her dad added with an encouraging lilt in his voice. "No one wants to visit San Francisco in January anyway!"

Allie was just about to tell them how Courtney was dying to escape the sun and the desert heat, when her mom reached over and patted her dad's hand. And Allie didn't say a word, because it wouldn't have mattered.

That hand-patting thing was a show of solidarity.

It was their silent way of saying they agreed with each other.

And it meant one important thing: This conversation was over.

Allie pushed her plate away. "May I be excused?"

Her mom raised an eyebrow, first at the half-eaten pizza, and then at Allie. "Don't be mad at us."

She wasn't mad. She was disappointed. And she was having a hard time hiding it.

As she was leaving the kitchen, she heard her mom's voice behind her. "If you want Courtney to visit so badly, figure out a way to get her here."

They couldn't see her roll her eyes as she left with Bo right on her heels, like he always was.

Inside her room, she flopped down on her bed and FaceTimed Courtney. When she answered, the look on her face said it all.

"No?" Allie guessed.

"Yep. You?"

"Same." Allie sucked in a breath. "My mom said you're welcome to come, but we have to figure out a way to get you here ourselves. So, I don't know, maybe you'll sprout wings in your sleep tonight."

"Yeah, I'm sure that'll happen. Hey, and if not, maybe I'll stumble on a secret teleportation device or something. There's this suspicious-looking shack behind the cafeteria that I've been meaning to check out. Could be a portal."

"Who knows? It's possible."

"As possible as me sprouting wings in my sleep."

Then Allie's phone chirped. She read the screen.

Maddie

Did you finish math?
I'm stumped on #12

"I've gotta go," Allie said to Courtney. "Maddie has a homework question."

"Okay. Tell her I said hi," Courtney said.

"I will. And I'll ask her if she has any ideas for us."

But Maddie didn't. And after they started a group chat to discuss it, neither did Emma or Zoe. Her best friends promised to think about it, but it seemed impossible, and by the time Allie crawled into bed that night, she felt frustrated beyond belief.

Allie was about to drift off to sleep, when her phone buzzed. She groaned as she rolled to one side, reached for it on the nightstand, and peeled one eye open.

Courtney

We didn't finish good
day/bad day!

Allie blinked fast, trying to force herself to wake up. She had to reply. She couldn't break their streak.

> I got to level 26 in Destination Earth
> My room is only 80 degrees right now
> Thinking of visiting you made me SO happy

> You live too far away
> Summer is too far away
> I can't wait to be your roommate again!

Allie felt a pang of guilt, but she pushed it down. The hackathon wasn't going to happen anyway. Chances were, she'd be spending the summer with Courtney. What was the point of telling her about the application?

She had already recapped her good day, so she went straight to her bad day list:

Allie

> Being far away from your best friend sucks
> I'm all out of gummy worms
> I'm not going to Game On without you!

Allie wanted that last one to be true. But she was totally out of ideas.

monday

three

Allie rested her lunch tray against her hip and scanned the quad. She took a deep inhale. The rain had left everything feeling clean and new, but she was glad the sun was out again.

She walked toward her friends, all gathered around their table underneath the big oak tree. Maddie and Chris were sitting next to each other on one side, and Zoe and Emma were across from them. Zoe scooted over to make room next to her, and Allie squeezed in.

"Missed you on the bus this morning," Zoe said as she popped a chip in her mouth. "Where were you?"

"My dad had a meeting downtown, so he dropped me off on the way." Allie ripped into her sandwich wrapper. She'd started to take a bite, when she realized Zoe was staring at her.

"What?" Allie asked.

Zoe leaned in closer. "I don't think I was the only one who missed you."

Marcus? she mouthed, feeling the blood rush to her chest and her cheeks and the tips of her ears.

Zoe nodded.

"Why? Did he say something?"

"Not exactly," Zoe whispered. "But when you didn't get on the bus at your stop, he kept turning around and looking in my direction, like he was trying to figure out where you were. Apparently, that boy can't start his day without your daily, *Hey-six, hey-three* routine." Zoe said it using a high-pitched voice for Allie and a lower one for Marcus.

"We do not sound like that."

"Oh, you totally do."

Just when Allie thought they might go back and forth like that for the entire lunch period, Emma leaned forward to get their attention. "Did you show Allie the video from the soccer game yesterday?"

Zoe immediately seemed to forget the Marcus thing. "You *have* to see this. I was going to show you on the bus. It is *hil-ar-i-ous!*" Zoe looked to be sure Mr. Mohr wasn't walking around with his orange bucket, confiscating devices, then she pulled her phone from her back pocket.

"Remember that kick I took in the ribs? Check it out. Emma's mom caught the whole thing on video."

The rest of the group crowded around, and Zoe pressed PLAY.

On the screen, a girl wearing a #22 Raptors jersey kicked the ball loose from Emma and took off, dribbling it straight for their goal. Zoe crouched down low, ready to block it.

Raptor #22 took a few steps, planted her left foot, and swung her right leg back, preparing to kick it with everything she had. But then Zoe lurched forward, throwing her whole body on top of the ball, and #22's foot landed right in her ribs instead.

Everyone around the table winced.

"No, wait," Zoe said, holding up her finger. "You've gotta hear it, too. The best part is the noise I make. I swear, it's not even human!"

Emma pressed PLAY again. Everyone tried to move closer to the phone, but it was impossible to hear with all the noise in the quad.

"Hold on." Zoe reached into her backpack and pulled out a pair of blue-and-gray earbuds, shaking them out to untangle the cord. She handed one side to Maddie and the other to Allie.

"When did you get these?" Maddie asked. "I thought you were saving for those wireless Beats?"

"I was," Zoe said. "But these were on sale after Christmas, so I caved. I can't stand that cord, though."

"Return them," Emma said.

"Tried. Can't. Sale items are final." She pressed PLAY. "Okay, listen."

Maddie and Allie watched and listened. This time, they could hear the dive. The kick. And the low, guttural, inhuman-sounding groan that came out of Zoe's mouth.

"Yikes," Maddie said.

"Brutal," Allie added.

Zoe shook her head. "Eh. Goalie life. You know what they say: 'No grass stains, no glory. No bruises, no story.'"

For the next ten minutes, they chatted about their latest Netflix obsession and speculated about how long the newest celebrity couple would last. And then Allie finished her sandwich, downed her water, and tossed her unopened bag of chips to Emma.

"Want these?" she asked.

"Duh," Emma answered, ripping the bag open.

"I've got to run." Allie gathered up her trash. "We're getting a new assignment in Advanced Computer Science today, and I want to get a head start."

She glanced over at the basketball courts. Nathan Frederickson was there, sitting at his usual table on the blacktop with his friends, Cory and Mark. He still spent some lunches in the computer lab, but Allie couldn't remember the last time she had to drag him out of there and into the sunlight. As she was watching, he stood, reached for a basketball, and passed it to Cory.

Good, Allie thought. She wanted to get to the lab first.

For weeks, Ms. Slade had been hinting about this assignment. She promised it would be the biggest challenge yet, but totally unique and lots of fun. Allie couldn't wait. She was always excited about new projects. And she was always excited about a new opportunity to beat Nathan.

"What are you building this time?" Zoe asked. "Is it a game?"

"Or an app?" Emma asked.

"What's the theme?" Maddie asked.

"Do we get to play?" Chris asked.

"I don't know, but I'm about to find out!" Allie threw her wrappers in the closest trash can and took off for the lab, waving over her shoulder as she called, "See you later!"

four

Allie speed-walked into the lab and fell into her seat. She had started the school year in the first row of her CS class, right in front of Ms. Slade's desk, but she'd moved to the back of the room and took the empty seat next to Nathan when the two of them were working together on their entries for the Games for Good youth coding competition. She could have moved back to her original computer station, but she decided she liked it in the back, so that's where she stayed.

She fired up her computer and logged in to the server to check on Click'd, like she always did at the beginning of class. A few clicks later, she was looking at the stats.

Everything looked good. She quickly deleted a few obviously fake accounts and checked over the crash reports and error logs, but there was nothing out of the ordinary.

Click'd didn't require too much of her attention anymore. It had been going strong for nearly four months. She now had just a little more than two thousand users across the country, and it was starting to grow to new schools in new areas.

Right as the bell rang, Nathan collapsed into the seat next to her.

"Hey, Gator," he said as he fired up his computer and logged in. She gave him a chance to check on his stats before she asked for an update on Built.

He angled the monitor so she could see what he was seeing. "A little better. I added a few new items to the general store and sped everything up a bit, so houses get built a little faster. Minor stuff. We'll see if it makes the numbers start climbing again."

Nathan had been a finalist in Games for Good, just like Allie had been, only his game didn't self-destruct two days before the show, so he got to be on stage, demo to hundreds of important people, and get the attention of the Spyglass Games executive team. For a while, he'd been a little bit famous. His name and his picture were all over the news, he was featured in a bunch of stories about kid coders, and he even got to be on the local TV news station.

But over the last month or so, his user base had been declining, and Nathan couldn't explain why. Neither could anyone at Spyglass Games. They'd told him to tweak a few things here and there and see if it made a difference, but so far it hadn't.

"Maybe Naomi Ryan will have some new ideas for you during your meet-and-greet?"

Nathan started to say something else, but then he looked around at the room, now almost filled with students, and seemed to change his mind.

The lab door flew open and Ms. Slade breezed in with a bright "Good afternoon, everyone!" Her hair was piled into a bun at the top of her head with a yellow pencil holding it in place. She was wearing jeans, a bright orange sweater, and dark green earrings. Allie squinted, trying to get a look at them, but she couldn't tell what they were from that distance.

That was one thing she missed about sitting at the front of the class. Ms. Slade had a huge collection of earrings she'd made on the computer lab's 3-D printer—power tools, keyboard keys, music notes—and she always matched them with the current project theme.

She walked back to her desk and picked up a red bucket. She lifted it in the air, reached inside, and removed a blue Lego block. "Okay, who's ready for the next big assignment?"

Ms. Slade scooped up a handful of Legos and dropped them on Xander Pierce's desk. They sounded like the rain that had been hitting Allie's window all night.

"Build something," she told him.

Xander stared at the pile. "Like what?"

"It doesn't matter. Anything. Just build it as quickly as you can." She began walking around the room, desk to desk, dropping handfuls of Legos in front of each person.

Once she got her pile, Allie began snapping hers together. She wasn't even sure what she was building, but after a few minutes, she realized it looked a little bit like an airplane, so she went with it.

By the time Ms. Slade returned to the front of the room, Xander had finished building a house. Next to him, Jessica Morse had built something that looked like a car. Ms. Slade picked up their creations and held each one in the air.

"You've built lots of things in this class. And now, you're going to take them apart and put them back together again." Ms. Slade broke off the top half of Xander's house. And then she separated the bottom part of Jessica's car. While everyone watched, she reassembled them. "See. Now you've got something completely new," she said, proudly displaying her new creation.

"What is it?" Xander asked.

Ms. Slade studied it. "I have absolutely no idea. But now it's not a car or a house, is it? It's something else entirely."

Ms. Slade handed it to Jessica. And then she walked to the whiteboard, picked up the green marker, and in big, swirly letters she wrote:

REUSE!

"It applies to environmental waste and code waste, too."

Ms. Slade stepped into the aisle and tapped her fingers

against her dangly earrings. Allie grinned when she realized they were two green-and-white recycling symbols.

"The fastest way to build a brand-new app is to reuse the code you've already written. So, this time, you're being graded on speed. You have the rest of this week to build and test your app, and next week to release it to a real user base. It can be the entire school or a small group—that's up to you—but real people have to begin using it by Monday, one week from today. You'll have four days to gather data, and on Friday, you'll each present your app and tell us what you learned."

Allie could hear the huffs and sighs and "no ways" echoing off the walls of the lab.

"It's easier than you think!" Ms. Slade said. "Just look at all the games you've made in the past. Go back through your repositories. Look at everything you've ever written and ask yourselves how to you can turn it into something totally new. Share like you used to do with real Legos when you were little kids." She picked up the bizarre looking Lego thing she'd built. "You're at slightly different levels in this class, and some of the projects you've built might be more advanced than others, but you all have something you can share."

Ms. Slade gestured toward Allie. "Allie has code that knows how to pull pictures from Instagram; maybe someone here could use that." She walked to the other side of the room. "Maggie, you have code that translates voice to text. And, Tyler, you have code to make custom emojis."

She crossed the room again. "Nathan has code for creating a whole virtual city, and Francis has code for creating an interactive choose-your-own-adventure book. I could go on and on, but I think you get the point. There's no limit to the things you could build together!"

Ms. Slade scanned the room with eager eyes, as if she were expecting a little more excitement.

"And for those of you applying to Hackathon, this is exactly the kind of thing the admissions committee will be looking for: proof that you can write quickly, share code, and work as a team." Allie thought about how close she'd come to hitting that SUBMIT button on the application the night before, and her heart started beating faster.

Ms. Slade circled her hand above her head. "Everyone, take out a piece of paper and make a list of every app or game you've ever written. Then list each one's assets. Mentally tear your own apps into smaller pieces. When you have your list, I want you to get up and walk around the room. Tell each other what you have. Brainstorm. Work together. Use each other's code *and* brainpower."

All around the lab, Allie could hear people shuffling around in their backpacks and tearing pages from their notebooks. And then the room got quiet.

She leaned over to Nathan. "Any idea what you're going to build?"

He shook his head. "Not a clue."

Good, Allie thought. At least she wasn't the only one.

five

For the rest of the day, the reuse assignment was all Allie could think about. She kept picturing the list she'd made in class—which not only included the apps her classmates built, but also the ones her CodeGirls had made over the summer—hoping an idea would magically leap off the page and into her head. But by the time school ended, she still had nothing.

She gathered her stuff from her locker, swapping out her Spanish and science textbooks for math and history, and took off for the roundabout where Bus #14 was waiting. She climbed the steps and paused at the landing, just like she did every day.

Marcus Inouye was in his usual spot in the third row, leaning up against the window. He tipped his chin toward her. "Hey, Three."

"Hey, Six," she said, tightening her grip on her backpack strap.

It had been like that for almost four months, ever since Allie released Click'd, when Marcus took the number six spot on her leaderboard, and she took the number three spot on his.

She walked to her seat in the middle of the bus and flopped down next to Zoe.

"'Hey, Six.' 'Hey, Three,'" Zoe mocked, using the same voices she had during lunch.

Allie smacked her arm with the back of her hand.

"You know what you need?" Zoe asked.

"A new seatmate?" Allie said sarcastically.

Zoe ignored her. "You need a Marcus Plan."

"I don't have room in my head for a Marcus Plan. I'm too busy trying to come up with a Reuse Plan." And in the back of her mind, she was still holding out hope for a Courtney Plan.

"What's a Reuse Plan?"

Allie told her about the Legos, and the game she had to create and roll out in less than a week. It made her sweat just thinking about it.

"If you don't have to write it from scratch, shouldn't it be easy?"

"Sure, but I still need a good idea. That's the hardest

part, and everyone else in class already came up with something. Ava is making some geocaching game that's going to take people all around campus to find hidden boxes filled with prizes. And Ben is building an app to get people collecting objects for a time capsule. Even Nathan figured out what he's building."

"What's he doing?"

"He wouldn't tell me. But I'm sure he's got some killer idea. He was talking to everyone in class about taking parts of their code. He'll build something good, I know it." Allie felt that familiar adrenaline rush. "I need an idea, Zoe."

"Well, you came up with the idea for Click'd because you had a problem to solve, right? What's the biggest problem you need to solve right now?"

Allie didn't even need to think about it. "Getting a plane ticket for Courtney."

"Maybe the App Store has an idea for us." Zoe reached into her backpack. She tried to free her phone, but the earbuds were plugged in and the cord kept getting tangled up in books, pens, and candy wrappers. "Ugh. Hate. This. Cord." She finally freed her phone, launched the App Store, and scrolled through the icons, mumbling to herself. "Let's see . . . apps that make money. Money-money-money-money . . ."

Allie looked over Zoe's shoulder as the apps blurred by. Nothing on the screen caught her eye, but something else had: Zoe's earbuds.

She thought back to what Zoe had said during lunch,

about wishing she'd saved her money to buy the wireless ones instead. And she pictured that long list of assets she'd created during class. She'd been waiting all afternoon for one of them to leap from the page and give her a big idea, and suddenly, she had it.

Share | wear, she thought. *It could work.*

Allie picked Zoe's earbuds off the seat and held them in the air. "Do you still want to get your money back for these?"

Zoe looked at her sideways. "Why?"

"How much would you take for them?"

"I paid fifty." Zoe held her hand out flat in front of her.

Allie slapped it lightly. "You're not getting fifty. They're used earbuds."

"Barely used."

"Still used."

Zoe looked even more confused. "I thought you were saving your money to get a plane ticket for Courtney?"

"I am. Would you take forty?"

Zoe's eyes narrowed. "What are you up to?"

Allie scanned the faces on Bus #14 and then twisted in her seat, facing Zoe. "About halfway through CodeGirls camp last summer, we all got bored with the clothes we brought to camp, so we swapped all our stuff, all the time. It was like having one giant closet, right?" Allie was talking fast. "After a week or so, stuff started getting lost. And people wanted to borrow specific things but couldn't remember who owned them. And anyway, it all started getting super complicated, so just for fun, Courtney whipped up this simple app so we could share and track everything. She called it share | wear."

"Like a library, but for clothes."

"Exactly!"

"What does this have to do with my earbuds?"

"If I'm right . . . everything."

Zoe still seemed confused, so Allie leaned in closer. "I want to do an experiment, but I'll need your help. Would you sell them for forty bucks?"

"Sure. Whatever."

Allie came up on her knees and spoke loudly and clearly.

"Hello! Can I have your attention?" Everyone kept talking, so Allie had to raise her voice. "Hello!" she yelled, waving her arms in the air. The bus gradually got quieter.

"Hi." Allie gave them an awkward wave. "I have a pair of barely used earbuds." She held them high in the air so everyone, from the front of the bus to the back row, could see them clearly. "As you can see, they are blue and gray. They sound great. Zoe paid fifty bucks for these two weeks ago."

"Plus tax!" Zoe yelled as she came up on her knees, kneeling next to Allie.

"She's looking to sell them. Does anyone want them for thirty bucks?"

"Thirty?" Zoe whisper-yelled. "You said forty!"

"Trust me," Allie said. And then she raised her arm

even higher in the air, demonstrating Zoe's earbuds like a game show host.

"Do I hear thirty?"

It was quiet.

Too quiet.

People started looking away, returning to their conversations. Allie's heart started racing. She was just about to sit back down when Penny McCaskill spoke up from across the aisle. "What's wrong with them?"

"Nothing," Zoe said. "I just want to get wireless ones."

Penny thought about it. And then she said, "I'd take them for thirty."

"Penny has thirty bucks," Allie said, scanning the bus. "Anyone want them for thirty-one?"

"I'd pay thirty-one," a guy's voice called out.

Allie's head spun in the other direction, and she saw Ryan Shay's arm in the air. She pointed at him and said, "Thirty-one."

"Thirty-two." The voice came from behind her right shoulder. She turned and spotted Alex Jefferson up on his knees in the second to the last row.

"Thirty-three!" A voice called from the front of the bus. Allie spun around and spotted Marcus looking at her. "Thirty-three," he repeated. Allie grinned at him.

"Do you still have the case and all the unused silicone thingies?" Anna Sheridan asked from her seat in the first row.

"Yeah." Zoe reached down into her backpack and

39

popped up again. "Right here," she yelled, waving the black zippered case in the air above her.

"Then thirty-five," Anna said.

Someone yelled, "Thirty-six!" and another voice called out, "Thirty-seven!" and someone else hollered, "Thirty-eight!"

"Thirty-nine," Penny said from across the aisle.

Allie looked over at Zoe, silently asking for her approval. Zoe gave her a thumbs-up and handed Allie the case. She was about to start passing the earbuds across the aisle to Penny, when a girl's voice behind them yelled, "Forty!"

Allie's and Zoe's heads whipped around. Julia Sanders was on her feet, standing in the center of the aisle in the back row, waving her arms in the air.

Zoe bounced in place. "Now we're talkin'."

Allie held the earbuds higher in the air. "Anyone want them for forty-one bucks?"

The bus was silent. Julia was still standing at the back of the bus. And now Penny was standing, too. Allie was surprised the driver hadn't noticed.

Penny sat down. "I don't have it."

Allie addressed the bus again. "Forty from Julia. Anyone else want in?"

No one said a word. Allie silently counted to five. And then she slapped the back of her chair with her palm. "Forty bucks! Congratulations, Julia!"

Zoe coiled the earbuds cord, zipped everything into the case, and passed it to Allie, who passed it to the person behind her. The two of them watched the case travel to the back of the bus, seat by seat, until Julia waved it in the air. Then a wad of cash began making its way to Zoe.

A minute later, Zoe had the money in her hand. "Okay, what was that?" she asked, fanning herself with her cash.

"I know what I'm building for the reuse assignment."

"You're going to sell earbuds to people on the bus?"

"Nope," Allie said, matter-of-factly. "I'm gonna sell all kinds of things, and not just to the people on the bus . . . to the people walking home, and the people in carpool, too." She tapped a finger against the bills, still fanned out in Zoe's hand. "I'm going to start with Courtney's share | wear app, turn it into an auction game exclusively for Mercer students, and make a bunch of money. Fast."

A slow smile spread over Zoe's face. "For Courtney's ticket."

"Yep." The bus pulled to a stop and Allie practically flew out of her seat. "I'll text you later," she called over her shoulder.

She couldn't wait to tell Courtney. She pulled her phone from her back pocket, preparing to hit the call button the second her feet connected with the pavement.

Allie was turning for the steps when she heard, "See ya, Three."

She stopped. She'd been so distracted, so excited, she'd almost forgotten about their daily ritual.

She looked over her right shoulder at Marcus and said, "See ya, Six."

six

"Hey, guess what?" Allie asked as she raced up her front steps.

"What?"

"You're coming to California in eleven days."

Courtney sat straight up in her chair. Allie could see the posters on her bedroom wall in the background. "Your parents changed their minds?"

"I wish. Hold on." Allie balanced her backpack on one knee and dug deep, feeling for her house key, which was lost somewhere in the textbooks, notebooks, and stray papers. As soon as she opened the door, Bo was at her feet, jumping excitedly.

"Hi, buddy!" She closed the door behind her and collapsed onto the entryway floor, legs crossed, arms out. Bo jumped into her lap and licked her cheek.

"Hi, Bo!" Courtney called through the phone.

Allie kissed him on the nose. "Come on, let's get you a snack."

As Allie walked to the kitchen, she told Courtney all about Ms. Slade's reuse assignment and her big idea on the bus ride home.

"People buy and sell stuff at school all the time," Allie said.

"Mine too," Courtney said. "I bought half my games off kids at school."

"See? We're just going to make it faster and easier. Thanks to Click'd, I already have a user base. And we already have the perfect storefront."

"We do?"

"*You* do. You built it in share | wear."

"I do, don't I?" Courtney threw her shoulders back. "It's super simple, but I always liked that interface."

"It's clean and friendly, totally easy to use—"

"And share | wear knows how to display items—"

"Exactly. And it already has all the fields we need, like color, description—"

"Except share | wear doesn't have code for buying or selling. We'll need to build an auction engine."

"*Borrow*," Allie said. "Who built an auction engine during camp last summer?"

Courtney didn't hesitate. "Kaiya."

"Going Once," Allie said, snapping her fingers.

Kaiya's CodeGirls project was a game called *Going Once*. Items appeared on screen one at a time, and little characters in the audience held up signs with their bids. The game didn't really have a point, but it was fun and a little too addictive.

"It's exactly what we need," Allie continued. "We'll use that as the foundation—"

"And then snap on the share│wear front end—"

"And grab the Click'd leaderboard code—"

"And we'll have a whole new app."

Both girls stared off, visualizing it.

"We'll make money by taking a cut from every transaction. Like . . . five percent?" Allie suggested.

"Ten," Courtney said.

"No one needs a credit card, or to ship anything anywhere. We'll just swap everything at school."

The two of them stared at each other.

"Swapped," Courtney said.

"Swapped." Allie could already see the logo in her mind. Swap'd. Just like Click'd. It was perfect.

Courtney's face broke into a huge smile. "Hey, guess what?"

"What?"

"I'm coming to California in eleven days," she said.

"I told you."

seven

Allie took the stairs to her room two at a time, Bo racing behind her.

"Okay, what are we going to sell?" Courtney asked. She walked around her room, removing things from drawers and piling them on her bed.

Allie went straight to her shelves. There were rows of books, separated by pictures of her and her friends, and keepsakes she'd collected over the years. In one corner, there was a stack of spiral-bound notebooks she'd saved from all her classes. English. Math. Spanish. Science. She couldn't imagine anyone buying any of that.

She opened her jewelry box and peered inside. Some of the earrings and necklaces were special—presents from her parents or her grandmother—but they were also a few she'd bought at the mall with her allowance and hardly ever wore anymore. She picked out two necklaces and a mood ring.

"How about these?" she asked, holding them up in front of her.

"Perfect," Courtney said. Allie tossed them onto her bedspread and went back to opening drawers.

"How much do you think I can get for this?" Courtney asked, holding up a snowball microphone.

"I bet you can get at least fifty bucks."

"Done." Courtney tossed it onto her bed. "Okay, what else?"

Allie went to her closet. There was a pair of soccer cleats she'd only worn a couple times before she outgrew them. She turned them around in her hands and brought one to her nose to take a whiff. They didn't smell funky, so she tossed them over her shoulder in the general direction of her bed.

She looked through her tops, but she couldn't imagine anyone else wearing her clothes. She sat down at her desk. She would get decent money for her brand-new keyboard, but she just got it for Christmas and she loved it. Besides, her parents would kill her if she sold that, even for Courtney.

She dug through her desk drawers next, pushing aside her stapler and a bunch of stray bookmarks, paper clips, old birthday cards, and valentines she'd tossed in there and forgotten all about. And then she felt something at the bottom of the drawer.

"No way," she said as she lifted a white case into the air.

Courtney brought the phone closer to her face, trying to see what Allie was holding in her hands.

"Check it out." Allie unfastened the Velcro strap that held it closed. Inside, there was a white Nintendo DS, along with a bunch of tiny game cartridges, all organized in little mesh pockets. "This is awesome. *Mario Kart. Dragon Quest. Sonic. Kirby.* I forgot all about these. Ha, look—*Nintendogs.*"

"Oh, I loved *Nintendogs!*"

"Right? But this one," Allie said, holding up the *Mario Kart* cartridge. "This was always my favorite."

Allie slid it into the open slot and pressed the power button. The screen came to life with the familiar logo and that little song that used to get stuck in her head. Allie sat down on her comforter with her legs folded and her thumbs on her DS, just like she used to.

The graphics were old-school and unsophisticated, and she loved it. As soon as she brought her fingertip to the joystick, it all came back to her, that familiar feeling of dodging and weaving turtle shells and skimming across the road to try to capture a boost. She played one game, peering over at her phone every once in a while, to watch Courtney run around her room, opening drawers and tossing stuff onto her bed. She came in seventh place. She played another and came in sixth. And then another and took fourth.

"Okay, what do you think?" Courtney asked.

Allie looked up from her game to find Courtney's bedspread covered with stuff. In addition to the microphone, there were several game controllers, a pair of boots, three books containing cheats for games Allie had never even heard of, a pair of drumsticks, and two empty picture frames.

Courtney tipped her chin toward the phone. "Let's see yours."

Allie angled her phone toward her bedspread. Her tiny pile was pathetic, especially compared to Courtney's.

"Well, I see you'll be buying my snacks on the plane," Courtney joked.

"Don't worry, I'll find more stuff when we hang up. I just got distracted." Allie held her DS in the air.

"Well, that's going to be your highest seller, for sure. The DS plus all those games . . . I bet you can bring in at least fifty bucks for that." Allie wasn't so sure, but Courtney didn't give her a chance to argue. She was at her desk now, propping up her phone so she and Allie could see each other as they worked. "Let's get going. I have the perfect playlist!"

Allie sat at her desk, and Bo curled up on the floor next to her. She logged into the CodeGirls server and created a new file, and Swap'd was under way. They decided to build two different versions, one for Courtney's school and one for Allie's. That way they could run their auctions independently. The music played in the background, but the two of them were silent while they each copied code classes from their existing apps and pasted them into the new workspace. They stopped every once in a while to talk about the new code they needed to link each piece together.

Bo barked at the door when Allie's mom called, "I'm home!" from the bottom of the staircase, but Allie ignored her and kept going.

They worked and worked, breaking only for dinner and the short homework assignments they had to get done for the following day. And by midnight, they had a working app.

It crashed the first two times Courtney tried to upload a photo, but Allie tweaked the code to stabilize it. The leaderboard didn't seem to be calculating correctly, but that required a small adjustment in the algorithm—they could deal with it during their lab time at school the following day. Everything else looked slick and worked surprisingly well. It still resembled share | wear, but now it was a lot smarter. It knew how to process financial data. It had a countdown clock and recognized that the player with the highest bid at the end of five minutes was the winner. It knew how to tell sellers how much they made, buyers how much they owed, and Allie and Courtney what their 10 percent "transaction fee" totaled. Everything was automated.

As Allie watched the app come together, she began to imagine what would happen if Swap'd worked. Not only was it perfect for the assignment, it was perfect for her Hackathon application. Speed. Collaboration. It was exactly the kind of thing the admissions team would be looking for.

She could demonstrate it during her meet-and-greet with Naomi Ryan. And then she wouldn't even have to mention Click'd. If she was lucky, none of them would even *ask* about it.

The first time Naomi Ryan met Allie, she was standing at a kiosk, in front of a broken, failed game. That was the only way she knew her, as *that* kid. The one who blew it the day before the Games for Good Competition. The one who wasn't up onstage with the other nine finalists, because she had nothing to present.

Picturing that day, remembering how it felt to sit in the front row of that huge theater and see Nathan onstage with everyone else, made tears well up in her eyes. She blinked them away.

Last time, Allie had Naomi Ryan's sympathy. This time, she was going to earn her respect.

tuesday

eight

The bus squealed to a halt in front of Allie. She let out a yawn as she hitched her backpack over her shoulder, and the bus doors opened with a loud *thwak*. As soon as she reached the landing, she glanced over at Marcus.

"Hey, Three," he said.

"Hey, Six," she replied. She was smiling as she flopped down in her spot next to Zoe.

"You're ridiculous, you know that, right?" Zoe rolled her eyes.

Allie ignored her.

"Are you two ever going to talk to each other?"

"We just did," Allie said. "We talk to each other every day. Twice a day, actually."

Zoe's mouth twisted up on one side. "That," she said, waving her finger back and forth in the air between Marcus and Allie. "That does not count."

"Sure, it does."

"No, it doesn't," Zoe said. "To be honest, I don't know why he doesn't try to say more to you, but since he's not stepping up, you're going to have to."

"What else am I supposed to say?"

"I don't know, *anything*. Like 'What are you doing this weekend, Marcus?'"

"It's only Tuesday."

"Okay, then, like 'How did you do on that math test, Marcus?'"

"We don't have math together," Allie said matter-of-factly.

"You're missing the point."

"Which is what, exactly?"

"My point," Zoe said slowly, "is that you two are flirt-greeting, which is fine at first, but at some point, you're going to actually have to move beyond that."

"We're going to have to move beyond 'flirt-greeting'? Did you just make that up?"

"Yes, I did, and I like it a lot," Zoe said. "To move beyond flirt-greeting, you have to ask open-ended questions, so he can't answer with a simple yes or no. You have to ask something that requires a real answer, you know? Something that will get him talking." She nudged Allie with her shoulder. "Don't you want to talk to him? Like, really *talk* to him?"

"Sure, but . . ." Allie scanned the bus. There were too many familiar faces. Too many faces in general. "I can't. Not *here*."

That was part of the problem; Allie's only chance to talk to Marcus was always on the bus where *everyone* could hear *everything*. The two of them didn't have any classes together. At lunch, he was always with a big group of his friends. The few times she'd passed him in the halls, they were rushing to get to class before the bell rang.

"Forget Marcus," Allie said, changing the subject. "I have something to show you." She pulled her phone from her jeans pocket and handed it to Zoe. "Check it out."

Right before they'd called it a night, Courtney had quickly sketched a logo. She thought it was too rough, but Allie loved it exactly the way it was.

"That's Swap'd," Allie said. "Launch it."

Zoe touched the icon.

The interface was so pretty, just like Courtney's original share|wear app. Same white background. Same green accent colors. Same font. It was clean and simple, friendly and fun. Allie still couldn't believe how much they'd done in one night.

"Go ahead. Set up an account."

Allie peered over Zoe's shoulder, checking to see if the interface was as easy to navigate as she and Courtney thought it was. Zoe clicked on the pull-down menu, found her name, and verified her phone number. She checked the box, accepting the terms of use, and Swap'd had its first official user.

"Okay, now what?" Zoe asked.

"Sell something."

"Like what?"

"Anything. Like ... those." Allie pointed to Zoe's gloves.

Zoe interlaced her fingers together and pouted. "No way. I love my fingerless gloves. My aunt Kristen made these for me." She wiggled her fingers in the air.

"It's not for real."

Zoe turned her hands over, examining the dark gray yarn and the tiny pink and green stripes. She let out a sigh.

"Write a description," Allie said. "I'll take pictures."

Zoe peeled off her gloves, handed them to Allie, and then typed:

Super cute, super warm fingerless gloves, hand-knit with love by my funny aunt using my favorite colors. The ones I specifically asked for. Because they're my favorites. I love these gloves. Allie Navarro is forcing me to do this, and even though she's my best friend, I kind of want to punch her right now.

"There."

Zoe started the bidding at fifty dollars and Allie uploaded the pictures, and a few seconds later, there was a new item in the queue. Allie pressed the START button, and the timer at the bottom of the screen began counting down from five minutes.

Allie and Courtney had put a great deal of thought into the timing: Six back-to-back auctions, each five minutes long. Thirty minutes a day, once a day, and that was it. That would keep everything fast-paced.

"So . . . what? It's like eBay but for Mercer?"

"It's *way* better than eBay." She tapped on the screen as she explained the timing. "We'll manually manage each auction so there's always a variety of stuff—less-expensive items mixed in with higher-priced stuff, used things mixed in with new ones—something for everyone, at every price point. If you don't see something you want, wait five minutes for the next auction to start."

Zoe looked intrigued.

"And there's a leaderboard, just like in Click'd." Allie always felt giddy when she pictured the leaderboard. She loved the whole game, but the leaderboard was her contribution; a little bit of Click'd in a whole new home. "We didn't want to reward the people who made the most money or sold the most expensive stuff, so we wrote the algorithm to calculate the percentage increase from starting bid to selling price; that way everyone has a chance to win. The leaderboards are updated at the end of each auction, so it's dynamic."

Allie bid $75 on Zoe's gloves. And then she logged out, logged back in as Courtney, and raised it to $80. She went back and forth, raising it again and again, until she reached $100.

"Okay, now I kinda wish this was for real," Zoe said.

Allie reached for the gloves and slipped them onto her hands. "Wow, these *are* warm."

"You are not getting my gloves, Navarro."

Allie pointed at the screen. "Okay, this is the best part. Watch. Five. Four. Three. Two. And—"

Zoe's phone let out a *cha-ching* sound, like an old cash register.

SOLD!

Allie's profile flashed on the screen.

"Sweet," Zoe said. "Now what?"

"Nothing. We're all good." Allie clapped her gloved hands together. "I'm keeping these."

"Give me a hundred bucks and they're all yours."

"I wish," Allie said. And then she got serious again. "So, do you have anything you really want to sell? Because I could use the money."

"Wait, if I'm selling stuff, don't *I* get the money?"

"Most of it. I get ten percent of every sale."

"Well, in that case, I'll come up with something." Zoe held her hand flat in front of Allie and said, "Give me those. I think *way* better when my hands are warm."

nine

At lunch, Allie waited in line for her food and then went straight to the lab. She thought she'd have the place to herself, but Nathan was already there, headphones on, tapping away on his keyboard.

Of course.

The reuse assignment was just that: an assignment. It wasn't even a competition, but still, she and Nathan were competing against each other, because she and Nathan were *always* competing against each other.

She dropped her backpack next to her chair, fired up her computer, logged into the server, and navigated over to her Swap'd code, looking over everything Courtney had worked on during her own lab time earlier that day.

Courtney had cleaned up a few things, fixed the leaderboard algorithm, and run some more tests, and now, they were even closer. They might even be able to roll it out later that night, which seemed totally impossible if Allie thought about the fact that they'd had nothing but an idea less than twenty-four hours earlier, but totally possible as she looked over the code. It was solid.

As she clicked and scrolled and typed, she could feel Nathan watching her. She looked over at him. "What?"

Nathan took his headphones off and draped them around the back of his neck. "Nothing."

"Don't you have work of your own to do?"

"Probably." He leaned back in his seat and kicked his feet up on his desk. "You look like you've had, like, six cups of coffee and at least that many chocolate bars. How are your fingers even moving that fast?"

"Practice. Repetition. Hard work," she said without taking her eyes off the screen. "You should try it sometime."

Nathan smiled. "You're in a good mood. I take it you figured out what you're making?"

"Not 'making.' Past tense. Made."

Nathan slid his feet off the desk. "As in, you're done?"

"Cakes are done, people are finished." She couldn't help it. Her English teacher spit out that annoying grammar tip practically every day. "But if you're asking if I'm going to have a game ready to roll out tonight, six days ahead of schedule, then yes."

"Really?" he asked.

"Really."

"You built a complete app in twenty-four hours?"

"Yep."

"How?" His gaze traveled around the lab. "Who?"

Allie smirked. "Aw . . . are you sad that I didn't ask you for code? Or just surprised?"

"Neither," he said. "I couldn't care less. I'm just curious where you got it, that's all."

"My CodeGirls," Allie said. "How about you? Where did you get your code?"

He shrugged. "Places. People." He pointed at her monitor. "Give me a demo?"

She pointed at his monitor. "Demo yours."

"I asked you first."

Allie didn't want to play this game with him. She had no reason to keep Swap'd a secret; in fact, she'd been dying to show it off all day. Allie threw her shoulders back as she twisted her monitor toward him.

"Okay, so Courtney and I started here, with this closet-sharing app she created last summer called share|wear. Then we figured out what else we needed." She pointed to another collection of code. "That's Kaiya's auction engine. And that's Jayne's calculation engine." She kept going, pointing out clusters of code on the screen and identifying the original source. "We used my backend database and leaderboard code from Click'd, snapped it all together, and . . . we were done."

"Finished."

"Yeah, whatever." She pulled her phone from her pocket and handed it to him. "It's called Swap'd."

"What does it do?"

"Click on it. You'll see."

Nathan clicked on the icon and the Swap'd interface came to life.

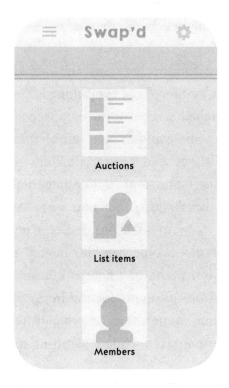

She walked him through the game, just like she had with Zoe. "We'll hold auctions every day after school from three thirty to four," Allie said.

"Why three thirty?"

"Well, because Courtney and I have to be online to monitor and manage everything, but I have soccer practice three days a week, Courtney has volleyball, and we both have homework. And it's an hour later in Arizona. This way, Courtney can go to her school's computer lab right before volleyball practice, and I can monitor everything during the bus ride home."

"A captive audience," Nathan said.

"Exactly."

He leaned back in his chair and folded his arms. "It looks like you've thought of everything."

Allie switched screens until they were looking at the empty queue. She couldn't help but picture it filled with clothes, and shoes, and games, all kinds of stuff. "Well, not everything." She tapped her fingernail against the glass. "We haven't figured out how we're going to do the exchanges on campus. We decided to use my locker to collect the cash—people can slip money through those little vents—but we haven't figured out how to set up the pickup and drop-off points for the items yet. We need a secure location. Somewhere sellers can leave their stuff without it getting taken while it's waiting to be picked up by the buyers."

Allie had been thinking about that part all day. She was

willing to give up her locker, but none of her friends were willing to give up theirs. The code might be solid, but no pickup/drop-off point, no Swap'd.

She changed the subject. "Your turn. What are you doing for the reuse assignment?"

"It's a secret."

"What do mean?"

"A secret? It's this information you know but you don't tell anyone else."

She looked at him sideways. "You're seriously not telling me."

Nathan shook his head.

"Why not?"

He curled his finger toward him. Allie leaned in closer. "Because it's a secret."

She glared at him. "Fine," she finally said. "Don't tell me. You know I'll find out anyway. You can't keep secrets in the lab."

"Oh, I'll keep this one."

Allie wanted to scream. Instead, she put her headphones on, turned up the music, and went back to work, blocking him out of her mind.

For the rest of class, the two of them worked side-by-side, typing in silence. After a while, she was so busy setting up the queue, tweaking the leaderboard code, and creating an inventory screen, she practically forgot Nathan was sitting there, until he tore a page from his notebook and set it on top of Allie's keyboard.

Allie read it:

#860

19-36-5

She pulled her headphones off. "What's this?"

"My locker and combo."

"Why?"

"You're using your locker for the cash. Use mine as the drop-off and pickup point."

She stared at his neat block lettering. "Don't you need it?"

"I never use it," Nathan said. "It's nowhere near any of my classes. Really. Take it, it's all yours."

Allie pictured the campus in her mind. Her locker was in the four-hundred building, smack in the middle. His was out in the science wing, near the computer lab.

"The student garden is right behind my locker," Nathan said. "So, you could hang out near the fence and monitor the pickups during lunch."

It was perfect. "So why are you helping me?"

Nathan played with his pen. "The locker is just sitting there. . . ."

"Are you sure?"

"Positive."

She pushed her chair away, grabbed the paper with his locker and combination, and went to the front of the room to ask Ms. Slade for a hall pass. She returned, waving both in the air.

"Thanks, Nate." She stepped forward to hug him, but she stopped short. She stuffed her hands in the pocket of her hoodie instead. "I'm going to go set everything up."

"Want help?" he asked.

Allie stared back at him. "Don't you have to work on your app?"

He gave his computer a cool, disinterested glance.

Clearly, Nathan had this assignment completely under control. Again. Allie wished that, just once, he wasn't two steps ahead of her, making her feel like she had to sprint to catch up and keep pace. Why couldn't *she* be the one in front for once?

Nathan didn't wait for her to answer. He stood, kicked his chair in, and combed his fingers through his hair. "The latch on my locker sticks a bit. Sometimes you have to jiggle it a little."

"I don't need your help opening a locker, Nathan." Allie rolled her eyes as she walked to the door.

"Fine, then I'll just keep you company," he said as he took off for Ms. Slade's desk and came back holding a hall pass of his own.

ten

"I've never understood the purpose of lockers," he said. "Everything is on my computer." They turned into the four-hundreds hallway and stopped in front of Allie's locker, #405. Nathan slapped his hand against the door. "Why do you need this anyway?"

"For my textbooks and stuff."

Allie dialed the combination. When she opened the door, Nathan took a huge step backward. "Whoa."

Textbooks might have been somewhere in there, but the "stuff" was a lot easier to spot. There were flyers and forms, reminders about overdue library books she'd long since returned, wadded up papers, stray hair ties, and wrinkled notes she'd taken in classes that somehow never made their way into her backpack. And wrappers. Lots and lots of wrappers. Gum wrappers, candy wrappers, and even an ice cream sandwich wrapper wedged in the far corner. She had to stand on her tiptoes and put half her body inside to get to it.

"Gross." She held it at arm's length.

Nathan made a face. "How long has that been there?"

"No idea. I can't remember the last time I cleaned this thing out." Allie pinched the sticky wrapper between her thumb and forefinger, walked to the nearest garbage bin, and dragged it over to her locker.

Nathan pointed at one of the pictures on the inside of her locker door. "How old were you and Emma here?"

"That was third grade. Our team was the Tigers, and Em and I had those matching orange tiger socks." It was back when they went to different elementary schools and only saw each other during soccer practices and games.

She scanned the rest of the photos of her and her friends, plastered over every inch of space inside her locker door, documenting their friendship over the last four years. There were pictures of Maddie and Allie at a concert in the park last summer, Zoe and Allie at Six Flags with her family, and all four of them at the waterslide park for her birthday. She moved everything around, making space so she could see the vents. And then she closed the locker door.

Allie took three dollars from her wallet, folded it in

half, and slipped it through one of the openings. It landed on the other side with a soft thud.

"Well, we have our cash locker." Allie dialed the combo, opened the door, and scooped up the money. "Your turn."

The two of them walked the empty hallways, passing all the classes in session.

"I bet your locker's even worse than mine," Allie said.

"I'd have to keep six-month-old bologna sandwiches and rotten bananas in there to have it be worse than yours."

"Oh, come on. Mine's not that bad."

"Fine. Then go ahead. Guess."

"Let's see." Allie thought about it. "A bunch of those spiral notebooks you're always using, but they're all half-empty."

Nathan raised an eyebrow. "Or maybe they're half-full."

Allie stared at him.

"What else?" he asked.

"A bunch of old thumb drives. A few pens . . . some are out of ink." She snapped her fingers. "Headphones."

"When was the last time you saw me without my headphones?"

"Never. That's my point. Maybe you have an extra pair in there, in case you forget yours at home."

"I never forget my headphones," he said as they walked through the breezeway that separated the seven-hundreds and eight-hundreds buildings. "What else?"

"Popcorn," she said. "Empty, greasy microwave popcorn bags. Everywhere."

They arrived at the lockers that lined the eight-hundreds hallway and stopped in front of 860. Nathan dialed the combo and opened the door. It was completely empty.

"Where is everything?"

"I told you, I never use it."

She stepped in to get a closer look inside. There wasn't even a library book or an old, marked-up practice test.

"No pictures?"

He shook his head. "Guys don't tape pictures of their friends to their locker doors."

"Some do."

"Well, I don't."

There was something about the way he said it that made her wonder if there was more to it than that. She hadn't asked about his friends in a while, but she hadn't thought she'd needed to. When Built was still going strong, she had to force him out to the blacktop every so often, but now that things had slowed down with his game, he was always with Cory and Mark. She hadn't seen him hiding in the computer lab during lunch for over a month. Maybe even longer.

"Everything okay with your friends?"

"Yeah. It's not that."

"Then what is it?"

He looked at the ground. "It's just . . ." He reached for the string on his hoodie and twisted it around his finger. "It's nothing." And then he slapped his hand against the bottom of his empty locker. "I bet you can't wait to see this filled with stuff."

Allie beamed and did a little dance in place.

"We should get back. Ms. Slade's probably wondering where we are. And I need to get to work." He swung his locker door shut and started walking away.

Allie followed him. "Get back to work on what, exactly?"

"I told you, it's a surprise."

"But you know *everything* about my project."

"So?"

"So, you have to tell me about yours."

"No, I don't," he said.

"Come on . . . At least give me a clue."

"Well, it's . . . unexpected."

"And?"

"And unique. No one else in class is doing it."

"Yeah, and . . . ?"

They reached the lab door. Nathan reached past her, opened it, and stepped inside. "And it's a surprise."

eleven

When Allie arrived at the field for soccer practice that night, her friends were already there. Allie dropped her bag on the turf and started changing her shoes.

"Is it ready?" Maddie asked. "Because I found this really cute shirt I could sell. It still has the tags on it and everything."

"I'm going to post a bunch of books," Emma said. "And some slime. Because everybody loves slime."

"Thank you!" Allie said, lacing up her cleats.

"Ladies!" their coach yelled. "That's enough stretching. Get running!"

Emma stood and extended her hand toward Allie to

help her up. They all brushed the turf dust off themselves and took off for the track.

"I have no idea what I'm selling," Zoe said. "I turned my room upside down and I can't find a single thing anyone would want to buy."

"That can't be true," Maddie said. "You must have something."

"Well, I did find a huge pillowcase full of leftover Halloween candy under my bed. I'd forgotten all about it. Think anyone will buy *that*?"

"Ew," Emma said.

"Ew," Maddie echoed.

"How bad can Halloween candy get in three months?" Zoe asked.

"Um, isn't *bad* bad enough?" Maddie asked.

"I'm doing it," Zoe said. "I'll even let them have the pillowcase. It's got little rainbows and unicorns all over it."

"Unicorns?" Maddie asked. "Are you sure that candy is from *last* Halloween?"

"Actually, no." Zoe shrugged. "To be totally honest I'm not sure how long it's been there. It could be from a few years ago."

"Ew. Again!" Maddie said.

"Someone will buy it!" Emma said. "If one of the popular kids bids on it, you'll start a full-on candy war."

"That's going to happen anyway, with all the stuff," Maddie said with confidence.

Allie shot her a look. "Really? You think."

"Sure. All the popular kids will just bid on one another's stuff, and the rich kids will battle over the expensive stuff. But whatever . . . It doesn't matter. The whole point is for you to make money."

The four of them kept running side by side, bending into the next turn.

The point was to make money, but it wasn't the *whole* point. Allie still wanted to create a game people wanted to play. Something that would be fun for everyone, like that first auction on Bus #14 had been.

"But I don't *want* it to be that way. That's why Courtney and I set up the leaderboard the way we did, so it wasn't just a popularity contest."

"The popular kids will still dominate the leaderboard, Allie," Maddie said.

Zoe nodded.

"Yep. There's no way to prevent it unless no one knows who the popular kids are," Emma said. And then she slowed to a stop. The rest of them stopped, too. "Unless everyone was anonymous."

"Avatars?" Allie asked.

"Avatars," Emma echoed. "No intimidation. No cliques. You can have a secret identity. You can be anyone you want to be."

"No one will know who the cool kids are, or who the nerds are. None of that will matter," Maddie said.

"Keep it moving over there, ladies!" their coach yelled. They took off at a jog.

Allie pictured the Swap'd code. She and Courtney were so close to taking it live, and even the smallest addition could throw everything off, but this seemed too important. And it wouldn't be *that* hard to snap it in. They just had to do it fast.

As they ran past their bags, Allie peeled off from the group. "Cover for me," she told her friends.

When she reached her duffel bag, she crouched down and pretended to tie her shoe. Then she unzipped her bag, found her phone, and texted Courtney.

Allie

Who has code for
creating avatars?

"Okay over there?" her coach yelled. Allie gave her a thumbs-up, and then untied her other shoe and took her time retying it. She was about to join her friends on the track when her phone chirped.

Courtney

Rachel. Jayne. Shonna.

They all had avatars in their summer projects

Hang on, I'll text them

Allie stuffed her phone back into her bag and rejoined the others. Practice began, and for the next hour, she was too busy to think about Swap'd. It wasn't until the four of them were walking to Maddie's mom's car, when Allie remembered the text she'd sent.

Got it. Shonna's a genius!

Allie thought back to the previous summer, when Shonna was building the avatar engine during camp. She'd pooled everyone for ideas for hats, glasses, funny T-shirts, and different hairstyles. Allie marveled at the fact that something she'd helped brainstorm in the Fishbowl six months earlier was now about to be part of an app she'd be rolling out at her middle school.

I dropped it in, did a little tweaking, and voilà!

You're a rock star!!!

Allie showed everyone the screen.

"Guys . . . we have avatars."

Allie yawned. "What's next?"

It was only nine o'clock, but it felt like it was the middle of the night. Allie and Courtney had been sitting at their desks for hours, tweaking the code and testing it, over and over again. They were equally exhausted and impatient.

They had a game. They had a leaderboard. They had lockers set up to collect cash and deliver the things that sold. They had an administration area where they could check off items as buyers picked them up. Allie could barely believe it was all happening. Swap'd was real.

"We're ready to go. Nothing left but our secret identities."

The two of them were silent as they opened the brand-new avatar engine and scrolled through their options. Girls. Boys. Hats. Glasses. Tank tops, T-shirts, blouses, and sports jerseys, all in different colors and patterns.

A few minutes later, Courtney said, "Okay, check mine out."

Allie refreshed the main screen and found Courtney's avatar smiling back at her. She'd given herself long dark hair, round eyes, and a bright orange ski hat with a matching shirt. She'd named herself GamrGrl.

GamrGrl

"I love it! Okay, hold on, I'm just adding a finishing touch to mine."

Allie picked a girl. She gave her long curly hair just like hers. It took her forever to settle on a shirt, but she finally picked a bright blue tee with a scoop neck. She scrolled through the optional items, passing the sunglasses, and the baseball caps, and the scarves. And then she stopped on a gold crown. It was perfect.

And then it was time to pick a name. Allie glanced around the room, looking for ideas. Her gaze settled on the DS, still sitting on her bedspread and opened to the last *Mario Kart* game she'd played. She grinned as she typed in the name and hit ENTER.

Princess Peach

Courtney laughed out loud when she saw it. "Princess Peach? That's your secret identity?"

"Of course! She's always been my favorite of the eight racers."

Courtney giggled. "You mean twelve."

Allie picked up the DS and counted the racers at the starting line. She made the sound of a game show buzzer. "Wrong. There are eight."

Courtney's giggle morphed into that belly-laugh of hers. "That's because you've never gotten far enough to unlock the other four."

Allie checked the screen again. "Really?"

"Really," Courtney said. "See, all the more reason you should not be allowed to go to Game On Con without me! You don't even know the real true pain of leveling up."

"Fine. I am going to prove to you that I deserve to be at Game On," Allie said, waving the DS in front of the phone. "Before I sell this, I'm going to unlock all four of the secret racers."

"You have to tell me their names to prove you did it. And no cheating. You could google it in about ten seconds."

"Oh, I won't cheat. I'm going to earn GamerGirl's respect fair and square." Allie touched her fingertips to the glass, and Courtney reached back with hers. It wasn't a handshake, but it was close enough.

And then her eyes flicked back to her computer monitor.

"Courtney," Allie said.

"Yeah."

"This might sound crazy, but . . . I think we're ready to take it live."

Courtney sucked in a breath and shook out her hands, like she was releasing all the built-up nervous energy. "Are you sure?"

"We've tested it ten times. What do we have to lose?"

"Nothing, I guess," Courtney said. "It just seems so . . . weird."

Allie knew what she meant. It did feel weird, but it also felt right.

"Ready?" she asked.

"Ready," Courtney said.

"Three." Allie brought her finger to the mouse and hovered over the button that took everything out of development mode.

"Two," Courtney said.

"One," they said at the exact same time.

They clicked. And just like that, Swap'd was live at a school in Arizona and another in California.

twelve

Allie could have invited all 657 people in the Click'd database who said they wanted to be notified about new apps, but she'd learned her lesson. This time, she started smaller, carefully hand-picking a mix of boys and girls across all three grades who she thought might be the most likely to buy and sell.

She chose people she knew well. But she also chose some she didn't know at all, selected purely because of what she learned about them from studying the user data in Click'd. They were into electronics and video games. They were readers. They were into fashion. They collected things. She picked a few of them because they had after-school jobs or got a generous allowance and always seemed to have a little extra cash on hand.

Her phone buzzed at the exact same time everyone else's did:

GOT SOMETHING TO SELL? CHECK OUT SWAP'D,
AN ONLINE STORE EXCLUSIVELY FOR MERCER STUDENTS!

It didn't take long for people to start poking around. Soon, they were registering and creating avatars.

Zoe was already in the system, so her avatar popped up on the player's screen first. She'd picked a girl with white spiky hair, a black T-shirt, dark sunglasses, and the name SweetTooth.

Emma's avatar looked nothing like her. She'd chosen a girl with dark hair and straight-cut bangs, and dressed her in a white T-shirt with a peace sign on the front. She'd named herself after the leader of her Hogwarts house: Helga.Hufflepuff.

Maddie's avatar looked a lot like she did in real life, with long blond hair and blue eyes. She gave herself bright red lipstick and a matching red blouse. She'd picked the name Fashionista.

Allie had invited two guys from her math class, Nick Bannerman and Evan Cardoza. She didn't know them well, but they sat in front of her in math, and as far as she could tell, the two of them didn't talk about anything but video games. She invited a few kids from her science class, two guys from Spanish, and a bunch of girls from her PE class. She kept toggling back and forth between the PLAYERS screen and the backend database, chuckling to herself as she watched all the new avatars fill the screen.

A new player named RiskItBiscuit appeared, and Allie didn't even need to consult the database to see who it was. The avatar had bright red hair that stuck up in all directions, freckles across the bridge of his nose, and a black T-shirt with a bright green zombie on the front.

"Welcome to the party, Nathan," Allie said.

"It's happening," Courtney said. "I'm up to twenty-six users."

"Twenty-two here," Allie said. And then an avatar with thick black hair, a green tank top, and dark sunglasses joined. He'd named himself SurfSup. "Make that twenty-three."

Allie checked the database, then angled the phone toward the floor, where Bo was curled up next to her chair. "Aww . . . look, Bo," she said. "Marcus is even adorable in animated drawing form."

A few minutes later, the queue started to fill with stuff for sale.

Maddie uploaded a photo and a description of a blue-and-white-striped shirt, Chris posted a watch, and Emma posted a bunch of books and a tub of green fluffy slime she made after soccer practice. Zoe posted her potentially disgusting Halloween candy, and Allie posted a necklace, a silver picture frame, and the mood ring.

It didn't take long before the rest of the players followed their lead. Allie pictured them scurrying around their rooms just as she and Courtney had been the night before, digging deep in their desk drawers, poking around in their closets, shuffling through the junk under their beds, desperately searching for stuff to sell.

Soon, the queue was filling up. There were bracelets and necklaces, two pairs of sneakers, a bunch of used video games, a scented candle, a beat-up skateboard, a brand-new art kit, a deck of Pokémon cards, room spray from Bath & Body Works, four fidget spinners, and a clock someone had clearly made in woodshop.

As they appeared in the inventory, Allie dragged and dropped them, moving them all across the six auctions so there would be a mix of items in each one—expensive stuff, cheap stuff, new stuff, old stuff—something for everyone.

She couldn't help but notice that Nathan hadn't added anything.

"Okay, I did the math and here's where we are," Courtney said. "We'll hold the first auction tomorrow, the second on Thursday, and the third on Friday. Check out my estimates."

Allie switched screens and studied the queue. Next to each item, Courtney had created a field where they could manually enter an estimated selling price, and it would automatically calculate their 10 percent take. "We might make a hundred bucks by tomorrow?"

"Yep. And people are just getting started! Look, my queue is almost full. People are posting stuff faster than I can assign an estimate to it!"

"Same here," Allie said.

"At the rate we're going, we might even be able to buy my ticket on Friday instead of Monday!"

Until that moment, Allie hadn't been completely convinced that Courtney was coming in ten days. She'd thought about it, and talked about it, and pictured it, but the whole thing still seemed so unlikely. The last thing she wanted to do was to get her hopes up, only to have them squashed when the Game On conference rolled around and Courtney wasn't by her side. But now that they each had nearly twenty items patiently waiting to be sold, she let herself enjoy the possibility.

Allie sent out a message to all the players:

WELCOME TO SWAP'D!
FIRST AUCTION TOMORROW AT 3:30 SHARP!

Courtney locked her eyes on Allie's. "Tomorrow is going to be fun."

"Really, really fun."

wednesday

thirteen

The bus arrived, and Allie climbed the stairs, pausing at the landing to glance at Marcus. *Be cool*, she told herself.

They greeted each other in their usual way, but then, as she was walking to her seat, Allie heard Marcus say, "Have you heard about Swap'd?"

Blood rushed into her cheeks and into the tips of her ears. If her hair could blush, it would have turned as red as Nathan's.

"Yeah," she squeaked out. "Sounds fun."

And then she turned and bolted down the aisle. As the

bus started moving, she collapsed into her seat and buried her face into Zoe's shoulder.

"Wait." Zoe chuckled under her breath. "What just happened? Did Marcus just say something to you?"

Allie nodded.

"What did he say?"

Allie repeated his question without lifting her head.

"And what did you say?" Zoe asked.

Allie looked up at her. "I said, 'sounds fun.'"

"You said, 'sounds fun'? That's it? 'Sounds fun'?"

"I might have said *Yeah* first. I don't remember. It's all kind of a blur. Oh. My. God. Is he looking at us?"

Zoe glanced in his direction. "No. He's talking to Jack Amhurst." She tucked one leg under the other and turned, facing Allie. "Dude, he gave you a perfect opening. He tried. That's what we've been waiting for! All you had to do was respond."

"And say what?"

"I don't know, something like, 'What's the name of your avatar?'"

"I can't ask that! It's secret."

"Fine, then, 'Did you post anything to sell?'"

"I already know he didn't. I have access to all the data."

Zoe pretended to bang her head against the seat in front of her.

"I am not good at this, okay?" Allie said. "I'm absolutely *terrible* at this, and I will never be less terrible at this. And I don't get it. I can talk to Chris, no problem. I can talk to Nathan without sounding like a complete moron, and he's—" Allie stopped before she said the word "cute."

"He's what?" Zoe asked.

"A guy!" Allie said, shaking off the thought. "He's a guy and I can talk to him, but for some reason I freeze up the second Marcus looks at me."

"He's really nice. He's in my Spanish group and we talk all the time. You just need an excuse to get to know him," Zoe said.

"Fine. How?"

The bus pulled up to a red light and stopped.

"I don't know," Zoe said, staring out the window. "But I'm going to come up with something."

Allie was sitting at her desk, waiting for math class to start, when Evan Cardoza and Nick Bannerman walked in and took their seats in front of her. She smiled to herself as she pictured their avatars.

The first period bell rang, and the TV mounted in the corner of the room flickered to life. The short intro song played, announcing the daily broadcast as the camera zoomed in on the news desk.

"Good morning and welcome to your daily Mercer Middle School broadcast, KMMS. I'm your anchor, Maddie Ellerts."

"And I'm your anchor, Kyle Crane."

The two of them arranged the papers in front of them. The camera shifted to the left and zoomed in on Kyle.

"Our top story today is 'debatable,'" he said, emphasizing the last word.

"You mean you don't know the top story?" Maddie asked. She had that lilt in her voice that made it clear it was all part of the script.

"No, Maddie, I mean our top story is 'debatable,' as in our *awesome* debate team." The camera zoomed in on Kyle. "This weekend our debate team brought home yet another Mercer win after a shocking upset against our rivals, the Steinbeck Stallions. Three more events to go before the regional championships. Do you think they can do it, Maddie?" Kyle turned to her and shot her a cheesy smile.

"I do, Kyle. I really do!" Maddie looked right into the camera and held it for a beat. "And now, in this week's sports news—"

Maddie kept talking, but Allie tuned her out. It was too hard to concentrate on the morning report when there were twenty-two items going up for sale in only seven hours and twenty-six minutes.

She was lost in thought when Maddie's voice caught her attention.

"And before I sign off I just want to give a quick shout-out to Princess Peach." She rested her hand against her chest. "I, for one, can't wait to go *swapping*. Good luck today."

Kyle stared at her, but Maddie just grinned at him and said, "Back to you, Kyle."

It took him a second to catch up. "Um, thanks, Maddie."

Allie covered her mouth to stifle her laugh.

Evan and Nick looked at each other and then bumped fists across the aisle as the TV went dark.

Mr. Harmon walked to the front of the room. "Pop quiz," he said, waving a stack of papers in the air. He began passing them out, row by row.

Allie couldn't imagine taking a test. It was all she could do to sit still in her chair. She felt restless. Giddy. It had been a while since she felt that way, but it was still familiar. It reminded her of those first few days after she introduced Click'd, when people were running around with their phones in the air, tapping them together, and squealing out loud when they saw where they'd landed on each other's leaderboards. And even though nobody knew who she was this time, *she* knew. And she felt special again. For a little while, she'd forgotten what that was like.

fourteen

At the end of the day, the bell rang, and Allie sprinted toward the roundabout. She was the first one on the bus.

She flopped down in her seat, pulled out her phone, clicked on Swap'd, and navigated over to the PLAYERS screen.

Someone named RainbowDash logged on. And then 3DPea logged on. And then ElevenWaffles, and FlipFlop, and Buh-Buy, and ScrappyDoo joined the party. Within minutes, there were sixteen people logged in, waiting for the auction to start.

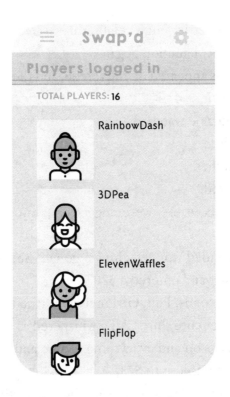

Players logged in

TOTAL PLAYERS: **16**

RainbowDash

3DPea

ElevenWaffles

FlipFlop

"They're here," Allie said as Zoe slid in next to her.

"Of course they are. There's buzz."

"There is?"

"Lots of buzz. Good buzz."

Allie quickly realized how quiet the bus had become. It was loaded with kids now, but there was none of the usual chaos. Some were chatting, and some were looking out the window, but a bunch of people had their heads bent low, staring down at their phones.

At three thirty on the dot, the bus started moving. A

bunch of phones let out a celebratory *ta-da* sound, and the very first Swap'd auction began.

Five items appeared on the screen, and the clock started counting down.

Allie and Zoe watched.

And waited.

And watched.

And waited.

Twenty-six users were logged in, but no one was bidding.

Allie decided to get things going. She clicked on Maddie's shirt and entered a $20 bid.

Within seconds, PonyGirl increased it to $21.

"It's a super cute shirt," Allie whispered as she increased it to $22. "Tags on and everything. Come and get it."

PonyGirl raised it to $23.

"All yours," Allie said as she clicked on the image of Chris's watch.

He'd started the bidding at $15, and LastPopTart had already raised it to $16. While she was watching, FlipFlop jumped in and raised it to $17, so Allie left the two of them to battle it out and moved over to Emma's item, where she found RainbowDash, ElevenWaffles, and ConeZone in a full-on slime war.

Allie checked the countdown clock: two minutes left.

"Aw . . . check it out," Zoe said, tipping her phone in Allie's direction. "They're fighting over me."

Seven players were rapidly bidding up the leftover Halloween candy that hadn't cost Zoe a thing and had been stuffed under her bed for who knows how long. With ten seconds left to go, Spider-Pig was winning with his $12 bid.

The clock ran down.

Three.

Two.

One.

The *cha-ching* sound echoed off the walls of the bus. And then the leaderboard appeared on her screen, displaying the top winners from the first auction.

Zoe was in the #2 spot. "This. Is. Awesome!" she yelled.

Some of the items ran their full five minutes without a single bid, and others got so many bids within the first few seconds that Allie had to keep checking to be sure everything was stable. It was. Swap'd worked exactly the way it was supposed to.

The next set of items appeared, the clock started counting down from five minutes again, and a new auction began. This time, a bunch of her own items filled up the little boxes on the screen. There was one of her necklaces, the silver picture frame, and the mood ring.

Allie watched all the items, but she paid special attention to hers, mentally totaling her take. Scattered *cha-ching* sounds filled the bus again, and the leaderboard filled up, replacing the players in the top three spots with completely different ones.

The Pokémon cards were a bigger hit than Allie had expected them to be. She'd estimated they'd go for $20, but the fight was fierce, and they were up to $30 with a full two minutes to go. ReginaPhalange raised it to $31, BubbleGumThumbs raised it to $32, and 3DPea was right there, raising it to $33.

The battle continued as the clock ticked down. Three, two, one, and *cha-ching!* They went to BubbleGumThumbs for $40.

A few people on the bus screamed, "No!" at the exact same time. And then they looked around, trying to identify who'd yelled, who they'd been bidding against. When they couldn't figure it out, they shrunk back in their seats, returning to their phones and the next auction. But the majority of the kids looked around, confused, noses wrinkled, shoulders shrugging, totally clueless about what just happened.

"Four more dollars in my pocket," Allie said to Zoe.

"That's it?"

Allie shrugged. "Ten percent. But, you know, it adds up."

It better add up to two hundred bucks, Allie thought.

The final auction closed, and the system automatically sent out a message announcing the winner of each item, followed by instructions for the buyers and sellers:

BUYERS: DELIVER CASH TO
LOCKER #405 BY THE END OF THIRD PERIOD.
PICK UP YOUR ITEM AT LUNCH AT LOCKER #860

**SELLERS: DELIVER YOUR ITEM TO
LOCKER #860 BY THE END OF THIRD PERIOD.
CHECK YOUR TEXT FOR THE COMBINATION.**

And then it kicked out a message to all the players:

**THANKS FOR SWAP'N!
NEXT AUCTION TOMORROW AT 3:30!**

The second the auction ended, the whole mood on the bus changed. The weird outbursts ended, and suddenly, all the players were holding their phones up to the others, gesturing toward their screens, and explaining what they'd been doing. The clueless ones began pulling out their own phones, clicking on links, and downloading Swap'd. By the time the bus pulled up to Allie's stop, a few of the people around her were already creating avatars of their own. Word was spreading. Everything was going exactly the way she hoped it would.

She jumped to her feet. "I'll text you later! I have to go see how Courtney did!"

Allie flew down the aisle, around the corner, and down the steps, completely forgetting to say good-bye to Marcus.

fifteen

"Daisy!" Allie screamed as soon as Courtney answered the FaceTime call.

Courtney reeled back. "What are you talking about?"

Allie held her DS in front of the screen proudly. "The first unlockable character is Daisy."

Courtney laughed. "You're playing *Mario Kart*? Now?"

"I had to do something while I waited for you to get home from volleyball practice. I'm dying over here. How did it go today?"

"*Ah-maze-ing!* I sold my microphone for fifty dollars and a video game for thirty. I only made about twenty bucks on my ten percent of all the other stuff that sold, but that's a hundred bucks!" She did a little dance. "How about you?"

"I made thirty-three bucks in my share of everything else that sold, so that's fifty-five dollars for me."

"One hundred and fifty-five dollars! Allie, we made one hundred and fifty-five dollars in one day!"

"Technically, in thirty minutes."

"Okay, what are you selling tomorrow?" Courtney stopped dancing and slid into her desk chair, all business, propping her phone up so she and Allie could see each other as they worked.

"I'm selling a bracelet and a pair of barely worn cleats," Allie said. "Emma is making more slime tonight, and Zoe went to the store today and bought more candy. Chris is selling a skateboard. And Maddie posted this super cute sweater, and as soon as she did, this girl named CrabbyPatty posted one too. I think Maddie is already starting to get some serious competition." Allie shook her head. "She is *not* going to be happy about that!"

"And you're selling the DS, right?"

"I've only unlocked the first driver!" Allie tilted her head to one side and stared at Courtney. "I have a bet to collect on, and I'm going to earn Gamer-Girl's respect first. Then I'll sell it."

"You know that was a joke, right?"

"I know. But don't worry. There's no rush. Check my

queue." Allie scrolled past the list of items people had already loaded into the system for the next day's auctions.

Swap'd

All Auction Items

Skateboard
Current bid: **$32**

Candy
Current bid: **$6**

Sweater—almost new!
Current bid: **$20**

Slime—my best recipe!
Current bid: **$3**

"I'm going to kill it tomorrow," Allie continued. "Look at my estimates. If everything goes as planned, I'll sell about three hundred dollars' worth of stuff. With my items plus the ten percent from all the sales, that puts me at fifty bucks."

"Mine should bring in about three-fifty, and with my stuff, that puts me at . . ." Allie could hear Courtney's keyboard clicking in the background. "Around seventy, I'm guessing."

"We'll easily have a hundred bucks by this time tomorrow."

"Or a lot more!"

"Exactly!" Allie echoed. "Add that to the one-fifty-five we made today, and we'll be at well over halfway there!"

Courtney gestured toward the stack of books on her desk. "I'd better get some homework done or I'll end up grounded next week and none of this will matter anyway."

She had a good point. Allie had homework piling up for all her other classes, too, and a huge Spanish test she hadn't even started studying for.

"Till good day/bad day," Allie said.

They bumped their fists against the screen and signed off.

thursday

sixteen

Allie had it planned. She'd been practicing in the bathroom mirror all morning. She was ready. She'd climb the steps, stop briefly at the landing, and then look right at him and say: "Hey, Marcus. Did you see the Swap'd queue today? There's a bunch of great stuff!"

Fifteen words. Far beyond her usual three. And then he'd say something, and she'd say, "See ya later," and walk to her seat.

"Easy peasy," she told herself. "You got this."

But as soon as the bus turned the corner and came into view, Allie wasn't so sure. Her hands felt clammy. She could feel sweat beading up on her forehead, and it was only fifty degrees outside.

The bus stopped in front of her and the doors opened, but Allie couldn't move.

Mr. Steve drummed his fingers on the steering wheel. "Are you planning to join us today?"

All the kids on that side of the bus were staring at her through the windows. She forced herself to take the first step, but her heart was pounding, and every limb was shaking. She heard Zoe's voice in her head, cheering her on. *Say anything. You can do it!*

She stopped at the landing, looked over at Marcus, and spit out, *"Es jueves."*

Marcus looked surprised. And then confused. "What?"

Allie was pretty sure the sweat on her forehead was visible. "Nothing," she blurted as she raced down the aisle and collapsed in her seat.

"What was *that*?" Zoe asked.

"I told him it was Thursday." She felt another wave of heat wash over her. "In Spanish."

Zoe started cracking up.

"Stop it. It's not funny. I had this whole thing worked out to say, but I totally panicked. What is wrong with me?"

The bus started moving.

"Look on the bright side!" Zoe said. "You finally spoke more than two words to him."

"No, I didn't. I said '*Es jueves.*' I literally said two words to him, they were just two different words. And they were in *Spanish*!"

Zoe couldn't stop laughing. "Why Spanish?" she asked with her hand over her mouth.

"I don't know. I have a Spanish test today and I was up late studying. I guess it was just some weird subconscious thing."

"Aw, but a cute weird subconscious thing." Zoe patted her leg. "I call that progress. Frankly, I don't know why you're so nervous. I mean, just because his hair is always shiny and he looks like a model for a shampoo ad—"

"Not helping."

"And because of those arms. Man, all those years of baseball have been really good to that boy."

Allie had to admit, his arms were really nice.

"He's got a good jawline. And that smile . . . with that little dimple." Zoe touched her finger to the right side of her mouth. Allie swatted at her arm. "Oh, come on, you know you're a sucker for that dimple."

"Please stop," she begged.

"Too bad you don't have Spanish with Marcus and me. You could stare at that dimple for a solid fifty minutes a day." And then Zoe got quiet. Too quiet.

Uh-oh, Allie thought.

Suddenly, Zoe twisted toward Allie and grabbed her arms with both hands. "That's it! I've got it."

Allie was afraid to ask. "What have you *got*?"

"A Marcus Plan." Zoe scooted over and tipped her head low. "Check it out . . . Yesterday, we took this practice test for our big verbal exam next Tuesday, and between you and me . . ." Zoe looked around to be sure no one could hear her. "Marcus didn't do so great."

"And you're telling me this because?"

"*Tu hablas español.*"

"Yeah, right," Allie said. "I don't speak Spanish any more than you do!"

"Sure, you do. You're in Spanish Two. Marcus and I are in Spanish One. Which means you're better at it than we are. You've taken all those tests before. I bet you still have all your notes."

Allie pictured the stack of notebooks on the shelf in her bedroom. She always saved her notes. "You never know when you might need them again."

"So . . . you can tutor him."

"Ha!" Allie said. "That's funny. Yeah, no way."

"Come on, it's a great idea."

"What am I supposed to do, walk up and offer to tutor him?"

"Of course not. That's where Princess Peach comes in," Zoe said, smiling and nodding. "You know how you said you can't talk to Marcus because you're always too shy? But Princess Peach isn't too shy. She's bold. She's confident."

"She's an animated character in a video game. She drives a race car in a ball gown."

"And, she can talk to Marcus anonymously, online, after she auctions off tutoring sessions in Swap'd."

Allie stared at her. "That's crazy."

"I know, right? Crazy and fun and *per-fect*."

"It's not perfect. It's . . ." Allie stopped short of saying *stupid*. And then, *ridiculous*. And finally, *terrifying*. She settled on: "It's not happening."

"Come on, chicken. What could go wrong?"

"Everything!" Allie said, staring at Zoe wide-eyed. "What if he doesn't bid? Or what if he does, and then someone else outbids him, and I'm stuck teaching Spanish to some other kid I don't even know?"

"He'll bid, I promise. I'll talk it up to him. He's in Maddie's math class, so she can drop hints to him, too. And Emma can . . ." Zoe trailed off and then threw her arms in the air. "I don't know, do something. It doesn't matter right now. The point is that this idea is awesome. You'll make some money *and* have an excuse to talk to him. It's your Reuse Plan, your Courtney Plan, and your Marcus Plan, all in one!"

"How many seventh graders do you know who are going to spend their own money for some total random to tutor them?"

"Not a total random. Princess Peach. And if you're in Swap'd, you're a Mercer student. And I'm sure if he asks his parents for money for tutoring sessions they're going to say yes. I mean, what parent wouldn't?" Zoe was getting more excited with every passing second. "It's perfect. Three days of online tutoring, totally anonymous. And then on Tuesday, when he gets an A on his test, you tell him, and you're the hero."

Allie didn't want to be a hero. She just wanted to talk to him without her voice cracking and her legs shaking and her forehead sweating. She just wanted to have a normal conversation with him. But maybe Zoe was right. Since she couldn't form a complete sentence in front of him, this was the next best thing. If she was anonymous, she had nothing to lose. If she sucked at tutoring and he failed his test, he'd never know who she was.

"It'll be easy," Zoe said.

"If it's so easy, you tutor him."

"I would, but dimples don't do a thing for me." She reached into her backpack, pulled out her notebook, and opened it to a blank page near the back. "Let's write it up."

seventeen

The bell rang, and right on cue, the TV in the corner flicked on.

"Good morning, Mercer Middle School, and welcome to the KMMS morning report. I'm Maddie Ellerts."

"And I'm Kyle Crane. We are excited to be with you on this cold January morning."

"It *is* cold, isn't it, Kyle? Makes me glad I have so many big, cozy sweaters." Maddie looked away from Kyle and right at the screen. "Speaking of sweaters, there's a really cute one today, perfect for all those *fashionistas* out there."

Allie tried not to laugh. Clearly, Maddie had seen the post from CrabbyPatty.

Maddie was still talking, but Allie was too busy looking around the room. She glanced at Nick, aka Buh-Buy. At Evan, aka ScrubHub. At Cassidy, who went by RainbowDash, and at Connor, who went by 3DPea. She noticed Marcie looking at her and smiled when she pictured her avatar named FlipFlop. Kira caught her eye too. She went by ReginaPhalange. They were all looking around the room, just like Allie was, and when they met one another's eyes, they each exchanged a grin, or a nod, or a small shrug—something that let the others know they were in on the joke; they all shared a secret.

But Allie knew a lot more about each one of them than they knew about her. She knew who had competed in the auctions the day before, who'd watched but never bid, who bid most aggressively, and who won. She knew each one of them wanted different kinds of things—Cassidy was into the slime, Connor was a sneakerhead, and Marcie was all about the candy. And she knew they all had one thing in common: They had money to spend.

Now she hoped they all had cash in their pockets and plans to deliver it to her locker before the end of fourth period. She didn't know if she could stand the wait.

As soon as the lunch bell rang, she raced up the stairs and into the four-hundreds hall, sliding past people, sprinting for her locker.

Maddie, Emma, and Zoe were already waiting there.

"Finally!" Emma said.

"Where have you been?" Maddie asked.

"I had PE! I had to run from the gym." She threw her arms around Maddie's neck and squeezed her tight. "Nice KMMS broadcast, *fashionista*."

"I am *not* letting CrabbyPatty take my business."

"Helloooo! We're all dying here." Zoe pointed at Allie's locker. "Open now. Hug later."

Allie's fingers were trembling as she dialed the combination—right, left, right again—and *click*, she pulled up on the latch and slowly opened the door. A bunch of folded bills fell out and landed on her shoe.

"Well, that's fun," Zoe said.

Allie unfolded the bills. She counted them. It was all there. She stuffed the wad of cash into her front jeans' pocket.

"I still can't believe I sold that shirt in just five minutes," Maddie said.

"My kitchen is going to become a slime-making factory," Emma said. "As soon as I get home from school, I'm going to make more fluffy slime. And crunchy slime. And slippery slime. And—"

"Need any help?" Zoe asked.

Emma's eyes narrowed on her. "Why? Are you trying to get in on my profits?"

"I don't need your slime profits, Emma." Zoe brought her hands to her hips. "I went to the store after school yesterday and spent every cent I had on candy. I have five more bags in today's auction. *That*, my friends, is called 'reinvesting.'" She put air quotes around the word.

"Hey, this is all fascinating, but can we walk and talk?" Emma gestured toward the eight-hundreds building. "We have to get to Nathan's locker."

They all started walking. Allie stayed behind. She cleared her throat and said, "Not *we*. Just me."

They all stopped and turned around.

"Why just you?" Maddie asked.

"Everyone's anonymous," Allie said matter-of-factly. "I can't let you see who they are."

"Oh, please." Zoe popped her hip. "It's not like we're going to tell anyone."

"This is the fun part!" Emma added. "We have to see who bought our stuff!"

"That's the whole point of avatars," Allie said. "No special treatment, remember? And that means no one gets to know anyone's real identity except me."

The three of them looked at each other.

"We just want to help," Zoe said.

"Exactly," Maddie echoed.

Emma pointed at Allie's pocket. "Let us take the cash. We'll divide it up and start distributing it while you monitor the pickups."

"Really?" Allie asked.

"Really," Emma said. She looked at Maddie and Zoe. "Right?" The two of them looked a little reluctant, but they nodded along.

"You guys are the best!" Allie handed Emma the wad of cash. And then she pulled a piece of paper from the side pocket of her backpack. "Here's a list with everything you need: Avatar name, locker number, and how much they get." And then she handed her a plastic bag filled with envelopes and a black Sharpie. "Fold the envelopes in half and slip them into the locker vents."

"Got it," Emma said.

"Go," Zoe said.

Allie waved over her shoulder and took off running for the eight-hundreds building. She hid behind the chain-link fence that lined the student garden, and peered around the corner, staying still, quietly watching Nathan's locker. He was right. She had a perfect view.

It didn't take long before a girl with dark hair pulled into a tight pony tail arrived. Allie recognized her. Melissa Carstens. Sixth grader. RazzleDazzle. She spun the dial, lifted the latch, and then, before she opened it, she checked her surroundings, like she was doing something sneaky. In one quick series of movements, she reached inside, grabbed the giant bag of candy, slammed the door, and scurried away.

A guy came into view and stopped. He must have written the combination on his hand, because he consulted his left palm as he spun the dial right, left, right. He did the same thing Melissa had done, looking around to be sure he was alone before lifting the latch. And then he reached inside and returned holding the tub of blue fluffy slime. He closed the locker and took off.

A minute later, Jason Fullerton arrived. He'd gone

to Allie's elementary school and she'd known him since kindergarten. He played percussion in the band, and she remembered smiling to herself when she saw his avatar name: Cymbalic-Gesture. He opened the locker and took Chris's watch.

The rest of the lunch break went the same way. Kids approached, often alone, but sometimes with a friend or two in tow, and dialed the combination. As they each took their items, Allie checked them off the list in the administration view. Twenty minutes later, Jessica Wilson stepped up and spun the dial. Jessica was an eighth grader. Allie had never met her before, but she knew who she was. *Everyone* knew who Jessica Wilson was.

"Hi, PonyGirl," Allie said under her breath. She wished Maddie could see who'd bought her shirt. She would have been happy.

Jessica took the shirt, closed the door, and walked away.

Nathan's locker was empty again.

eighteen

Allie and Nathan were sitting side by side at their workstations, but they might as well have been in completely different worlds. Headphones on. Music blaring. Eyes glued to their screens. Fingers flying across their respective keyboards. Neither one of them even noticed Ms. Slade until she tapped the top of their monitors to get their attention.

Allie slid her headphones off and dropped them on her desk. Nathan draped his around the back of his neck.

"My, you two are so serious," Ms. Slade said with a fake scowl. And then the corners of her mouth turned up. "Just checking in. How's it going over here?"

"Fine," they said at the exact same time.

"Great. Do you need any help?"

"Nope," Allie said, feeling smug.

Ms. Slade slid her gaze over to Nathan. His mouth dropped open, like he was about to say something, but then he looked at Allie. "Nah, I'm good."

Ms. Slade nodded. "Okay . . . How about your Hackathon applications? Need any help there?"

"All good," Nathan said.

"Same here," Allie added.

"Sounds good. I'll let you get back to your projects." Ms. Slade tapped their monitors again, and then walked to the next workstation.

Nathan leaned on Allie's side of the desk. "You're demoing Swap'd during your meet-and-greet next weekend, aren't you?" Nathan asked.

That familiar pit formed in Allie's stomach. "I don't know."

His eyebrows pinched together. "Why wouldn't you? It's everything they're looking for. Speed. Collaboration. Swap'd is perfect."

"I know it is. But that's part of the problem." She told him about her dilemma: Hackathon program, or Courtney and her CodeGirls. How could she use the game they'd built together to get into a program that would keep them apart?

"What about you?" Allie asked, changing the subject.

"What are you going to demo? This?" She craned her neck, trying to see Nathan's screen, and she almost got a good glimpse, but he was too fast. He grabbed his monitor with both hands, twisting it away from her.

"No peeking."

"Come on, this is nuts. I'm not going to steal your idea or anything. Why won't you tell me what you're building?"

"Because I don't want to."

"Because you don't *want* to?"

His whole I've-got-a-secret thing was kind of funny at first, but now it was starting to get to her. The two of them had always been competitive, but in a good way. This time, it felt different. One-sided. She'd told him everything, first about her game, and now, about Courtney. She wasn't keeping secrets from him. Why was he keeping them from her?

She was starting to wonder if all the success with Built had gone to his head. Or maybe he no longer saw her as his biggest competition.

Nathan just grunted.

"Well, I bet it doesn't do this." Allie pulled out a wad of cash from her pocket and fanned herself with it.

"No, it definitely doesn't do that." Nathan had a strange look on his face, but Allie couldn't read it. "Hey, there's something—"

Allie phone buzzed. "One sec," she said, holding up a finger. She peeked at the screen.

Zoe

Where is it?!?

Allie knew exactly what she meant. She typed back quickly.

Allie

I'm working on it!

Post it! What are you waiting for?

An earthquake

DO IT!!!!!!

Allie was giggling to herself as she slipped her phone back into her jeans' pocket. She turned back to Nathan. "Okay, you were saying?"

He shook his head. "Never mind."

"Oh, come on! Tell me."

"It's nothing," he said. And then he gestured back to his monitor. "Really. Forget it. I have to get back to work anyway."

Allie considered pushing him but decided against it. If he didn't consider her a competitor anymore, he'd wish he had. "Yeah, you definitely should. You better work day and night if you want to beat me on this one."

"Got it." Nathan tilted his head to one side, giving her a sarcastic grin and a thumbs-up. And then he pulled his headphones over his ears and went back to what he was doing. Soon, his fingers were flying across the keyboard again. He didn't look back at her.

Allie went back to work, too. She didn't have time to be upset about Nathan. She had an auction to set up. And there was still one more item to add.

She reached into her backpack and took out the piece of paper Zoe had ripped from her notebook on the bus that morning. She unfolded it and stayed hunched over, shielding it from all the curious eyes around her:

Want to take your Español grade from malo to excelenté? I'm the perfect tutor for you. I'll teach you everything you need to know to ace that next Spanish test and land an A. Three one-hour sessions. All online. Completely anonymous. Tu secreto está a salvo conmigo. (Your secret's safe with me.)

She read her post all the way through again. And again. And then she typed it up, added a picture of Princess Peach in her race car, and posted it before she had time to change her mind.

nineteen

Allie was all alone on the bus, hunched down low in the spot by the window where Zoe usually sat. She couldn't bring herself to look up and see if Marcus was there yet. She couldn't even bring herself to see who'd logged in.

"Is he playing?" Allie asked Zoe when she arrived.

"I think so. He's looking down at his phone, along with, like, practically everyone on the bus, so I'm guessing yes."

"Practically everyone?" Allie lifted her chin and looked around. Just like Zoe had said, almost everyone had their phone in their hands and their heads bent low.

Word was beginning to spread about Swap'd, both at

Mercer and at Courtney's school. Allie now had sixty-two users, and Courtney had seventy-three. It was building slowly, entirely by word of mouth, exactly the way they wanted it to.

As the bus pulled away from the roundabout, phones echoed off the walls with the celebratory *ta-da* sound, and the second Swap'd auction was officially under way.

This time, there wasn't even a slight delay before people started jumping in and bidding on the first set of items.

Maddie's sweater got the first hit, with a $20 bid from a player named BooBooBear. SuperGirl swooped in within seconds and increased it to $21. BooBooBear was back within seconds, upping it to $22, before SillyString stepped in and raised the bidding to $23. Zoe's candy was already up to $12. Chris's skateboard was up to $40.

The bus was quiet at first, but as the clock counted down to the final minute, the mood changed completely.

"Whoever Buh-Buy is, you'd better back off!" someone yelled. "That skateboard is mine."

"Then pay up!" another voice yelled from the back of the bus.

A girl two rows in front of Allie screamed straight into her phone screen and then went right back to typing in a bid, as if nothing had happened.

The people on the bus who weren't playing Swap'd had been looking around, trying to figure out what was going on, but now, they looked terrified. They kept making eye contact with each other, like they needed to join forces and strategize their escape.

A guy in the first row kept shouting, "Stop raising it!" to no one in particular.

Three.

Two.

One.

The cash register sound came from more phones than Allie could count. There were cheers, and high fives, and a few scattered obscenities.

"Here we go," a voice behind Allie yelled as the next auction started.

It was even fiercer, even louder. Every item had at least three bidders, and by the time the *cha-ching* sound filled the bus, everything had sold for well over its starting price. The leaderboard flashed on the screen with BooBooBear in the lead, and Zoe—aka SweetTooth—right behind her. A few seconds later, the next set of items appeared.

The next auction was even more fast-paced, with higher bids and even more competition, and Allie could feel the energy all around the bus. Players shifted in their seats, yelled, and sucked in their breaths. When the leaderboard appeared, a few kids jumped to their feet.

"Hey, settle down back there!" Mr. Steve yelled. "In your seats."

But Mr. Steve didn't have to tell them to sit. They were already back where they belonged, eyes glued to the screen, ready for the next set of items.

A sweatshirt posted by 3DPea was getting a lot of attention. There was another fierce battle going on over Zoe's candy. And just like the day before, RainbowDash, ElevenWaffles, and ConeZone were fighting over Emma's slime. Allie was so caught up in the excitement, for a moment she forgot all about her item.

When the *cha-ching* sound echoed off the sides of the bus, Zoe had sold her third bag of candy for $15. Zoe took the #1 spot on the leaderboard.

"Re-invest-ing," Zoe sang as she did a chair dance, waving her arms over her head. And then she stopped dancing,

interlaced her fingers with Allie's, and whispered, "Final auction. This is it. Marcus Plan in three, two, one."

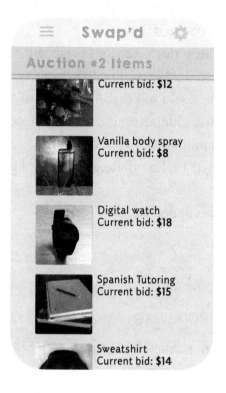

It was right there, filling the screen, big and bold and unavoidable. Starting bid: $15.

"I'm going to throw up," Allie said.

"You're not going to throw up."

"I'm going to die."

"Make up your mind. Are you going to die, or are you going to throw up?"

"I'm going to throw up and *then* I'm going to die."

Zoe tipped her chin toward the bus driver. "Mr. Steve is not going to be happy about that clean up."

The clock counted down.

Four minutes, thirty seconds remained, and there still wasn't a single bid. Allie could tell that six users were watching it. And she could tell that Marcus wasn't one of them. He was too busy bidding on the last bag of Zoe's candy.

"This is humiliating," Allie whispered.

"How can it be humiliating? No one has a clue who you are."

Finally, bids appeared.

ShakeItOff:	$16
DollaBill:	$17
DianaPrince:	$18

"Now we're talkin'!" Zoe said.

"I seriously feel sick."

"Why? This is exciting! You have three bids."

"Notice how none of them are from Marcus."

"Oh yeah. Good point."

"I can't look."

A bunch of guys in the back of the bus were screaming at each other. "What kind of wimpy bid was that?" one said. "Watch this. *This* is a bid!" another yelled. And then there was a chorus of "Oh, come on!" and "No way!" and "Who has that kind of money?"

A guy at the front of the bus stood up and yelled, "Would somebody please tell me what is going on?"

The girl next to him tugged on his shirtsleeve and showed him her phone. He returned to his seat and peered over her shoulder.

Allie was dying to know what the guys in the back of the bus were fighting over and how much she was about to make off them, but she wasn't about to take her eyes off her own item, especially now that the bids were coming in again.

BubbleGumThumbs: $19
LastPopTart: $20

That must have been more than BubbleGumThumbs and DollaBill could afford. They both dropped out within seconds. But DianaPrince and LastPopTart didn't seem to be going anywhere.

The clock counted down.

DianaPrince: $21
LastPopTart: $22

And then a new bidder joined the competition.

SurfSup: $23

Allie stared at her phone.

"He bid," she whispered. "He actually bid."

DianaPrince: $24
SurfSup: $25

Two minutes, ten seconds left. She watched the status. She couldn't tell if LastPopTart was no longer bidding or just waiting patiently for the right moment to pounce. The countdown timer kept going.

1:48.

1:47.

1:46.

The guys in the back of the bus were still screaming at each other. "Just let him have it!" one said. "Not a chance!" someone else replied.

Mr. Steve pulled over, stopped the bus, and stood in the aisle, hands on his hips, face bright red. "I said knock it off!" He waited there, staring them down until everyone had returned to their seats. The bus was quiet, but Allie could still feel the electricity bouncing off the walls, and the roof, and the floor. It was everywhere.

Mr. Steve took his seat, put the bus in gear, and pulled back into traffic. And right at that moment, another bid appeared:

DianaPrince: $27

"No!" Allie slapped the back of the chair in front of her, and the girl sitting there flipped around and yelled, "Hey!"

"Sorry," Allie said. She looked up to be sure Mr. Steve hadn't heard her. And then she turned to Zoe. "What am I going to do?"

"There's less than a minute left. Marcus might not be able to bid again without Mr. Steve catching him. You'd better see who she is. She might be your first student."

Allie switched screens, scrolling through all the user data until she found the name she was looking for.

DianaPrince
Kelsey Gilbert

Kelsey Gilbert. Allie knew her. She was an eighth grader, but they were in the same art class the year before. She was nice. And Allie couldn't help but appreciate her using Wonder Woman's secret identity as her avatar name. But Kelsey Gilbert, aka DianaPrince, could not win this tutoring item. She absolutely, positively, could *not* win.

Forty seconds.

Allie toggled back to the main screen. No one had made another move. Maybe Marcus was being smart, Allie thought. Maybe he was planning to hang back and then swoop in at the very last second.

"Wait her out, Marcus," Allie whispered. "Be patient."

The clock ticked down: 35 seconds. 34 seconds. 33 seconds.

DianaPrince was silent. Marcus was silent. LastPopTart was nowhere to be seen. Allie could tell there were two other players watching the auction, but they hadn't made a move.

Allie couldn't stand it. She toggled over to the administration screen and watched the auction from there, where she could see all the details, including the real names of everyone bidding and the people who were still lurking.

And then a new bid appeared.

SurfSup: $28

There were still six seconds left.

Five.

Four.

And then, without even stopping to think about what she was doing, she clicked on the clock field, highlighted the numbers, and typed a single zero. She hit ENTER.

Her phone let out a *cha-ching* sound, and so did all the phones around her.

"Yes!" The guy at the back of the bus jumped to his feet. "I told you!" he yelled, pointing at another guy two rows in front of him. Mr. Steve was trying to quiet the bus again, but Allie wasn't paying any attention to him. She was too busy staring at her screen in disbelief. What had she done?

SOLD

Marcus won. But, of course he had. Allie had just made sure of it.

Zoe grabbed her arm in both hands. "See! I told you he'd win."

Allie felt a twist, deep in her stomach.

But the feeling didn't last long. All the auctions were over, and the bus exploded with cheers, chatter, and speculation about who was who, and no one seemed to notice that the last auction ended a few seconds too early.

The leaderboard shifted, and new names appeared. Apparently, everyone had been battling over a Supreme sweatshirt, which sold for $82 and landed someone named HalfPipe in the number one spot.

The system automatically sent out a message announcing the winner of each item and followed it with the standard instructions for sellers and buyers. And then it kicked out a message to all the players:

THANKS FOR SWAP'N
NEXT AUCTION TOMORROW AT 3:30 P.M.!

The bus pulled up to Allie's stop and she jumped up as fast as she could, eager to get off the bus. She couldn't sit still with all that adrenaline coursing through her veins.

As she rounded the corner, Marcus said, "See ya, Three."

She stopped and looked at him, blocking out what she'd done. She threw her shoulders back, mustered up all the confidence she could find, and said, "See ya, Six."

twenty

Allie was sitting at her desk, studying the day's winnings, and waiting for Courtney to get home from volleyball practice. She glanced around her room at the posters and pictures of her and her friends, and then her gaze settled on her bookcase.

Up on the top shelf, in the far-right corner, she spotted the collection of spiral-bound notebooks she'd saved from every class since fifth grade. She grabbed the green notebook with SPANISH I written in black Sharpie and sat down on her bed with her legs crossed. Bo jumped up and settled in next to her.

She turned the pages, looking over the notes she'd

taken the year before, scanning the dates at the top, until she reached January. She'd drawn a line down the center of the page, dividing it into two columns. On the left side, there was a short list of questions in Spanish, and on the right, a long list of regular household objects.

"I remember this test," Allie said. Bo grunted and turned onto one side so she could pet his tummy. "I had to stand in front of the class while Señor Flores asked me all these questions. It was terrifying."

Allie read over the list, translating each item: Wrench. Chair. Train schedule. Cup. Bread. Flashlight. Shampoo. Apple. Balloon.

Her phone rang, jolting her back to reality.

"I made *bank* today!" Courtney screamed, her face the perfect mix of pride and elation. "The boots only went for twenty-five, but my second controller went for twenty, and the games brought in ten each, so that plus my ten percent brought me to one hundred and sixteen dollars!"

"I didn't do as well. Only bought in forty-two dollars."

"That's okay. Together we made a hundred and fifty-eight." Courtney's enthusiasm was as contagious as usual. "Add that to yesterday's take, and . . . we made three hundred and thirteen dollars! We're nearly there!"

"Not bad for two days!" Allie reached for her water bottle. She tipped her head back and took a big sip.

"Let me see what you sold!" Courtney said. Allie could hear her keyboard in the background. "What's this tutoring thing?"

Allie almost spit out her water.

"Oh, it's silly. Zoe has Spanish with Marcus and apparently, he's not doing very well, so she talked me into auctioning off anonymous tutoring sessions." She laughed nervously. "She thinks if I get to know him over the phone, I won't trip over my tongue every time I try to talk to him in person."

"Who's Marcus?" Courtney asked.

"What do you mean 'Who's Marcus?'" Allie looked right at the screen. "The cute guy from my bus. I've told you about Marcus."

"Nope."

"Of course I have."

"Not a word."

Allie thought about it. She must have said *something* about him at some point, during some good day/bad day exchange at the very least. She told Courtney *everything*.

"You know . . . Marcus. With the great hair and the cute dimple. We clicked, remember? I'm his number three. He landed on my leaderboard at number six and I've been trying to talk to him ever since. Zoe gives me a hard time about it practically every day."

"News to me."

"Not possible."

"Completely possible, and absolutely true."

"Wow. Okay, whatever. The point is that Marcus, who is *totally* adorable, bought three anonymous tutoring sessions, and we're twenty-eight dollars richer." Allie clicked over to her administration screen and changed the subject. "Look at my queue for tomorrow's auction. It's already packed. By Monday, we'll have more than enough to buy your ticket."

Allie barely had the sentence out, when her phone chirped.

Nathan

Can you come over?

I need your help with something

Allie checked the time. Her mom wouldn't be home for another hour and Bo needed a walk anyway. Maybe he was finally going to show her what he'd been working on.

"I've gotta go," she told Courtney. "Talk tonight?"

"Like always," Courtney said.

When they hung up, Allie typed a reply to Nathan.

Allie

I'll be there in 20

twenty-one

Allie put on her running clothes, laced her shoes, and grabbed her earbuds. Bo always had a sixth sense about these things, and when she got downstairs, he was already standing in the entryway, sitting politely in front of the coat rack, peering up at his leash.

"Well, someone's ready." Bo's tail swept across the hardwood floor excitedly. "Want to go play with Archie?" His tail wagged even faster.

They left the house and took off at a jog, heading for Nathan's. She ran past the corner store and the Laundromat, past her family's favorite restaurant and the little bookstore. Past clothing boutiques and the hardware store.

Two blocks later, the shops ended, and she was back among the brightly painted, tightly packed houses. She rounded the corner, ran up a hill, and turned down Nathan's street. When she reached his door, she was panting, sweating, and parched.

She knocked. Nathan opened it right away. "Wow, you got here fast."

Allie tapped her finger against her throat. "Water."

Nathan stepped inside, and Allie followed him into the kitchen. He walked straight to the sliding glass door and opened it so the dogs could play in the backyard, and then took a glass from an upper cabinet, filled it with water, and handed it to her.

He leaned back against the counter. "I didn't think you'd race over here for me."

Allie drank her water and took her time responding. "Excuse me. I did not 'race over here for you,' Nathan. I ran. It's called exercise."

He gave her a dismissive head tilt, like he didn't want to get into it. "Well, thanks for coming."

"Sure. What's up?"

"I have something to show you."

"Are you finally going to tell me what you're working on?"

Nathan didn't answer her. He just curled his finger in the air and headed for the staircase. She followed him into his room.

It had only been a month since Allie had been there, but it looked completely different. Last time, the bed was unmade, there were clothes strewn all over the floor, and his desk was covered with stray papers, soda cans, and candy wrappers. This time, it was clean. She could actually see the hardwood floor. His bed was made, his bookcase was neatly organized, and there was nothing on his desk but his monitor and a keyboard. She remembered the posters from last time—funny sayings, video game artwork, and one of his favorite bands. Over his desk was a poster that read THERE'S NO PLACE LIKE 127.0.0.1.

The largest wall was covered with memorabilia from Games for Good, including the sign from his Built kiosk, autographed by all the judges, even Naomi Ryan.

Looking at it made her sad. Allie had loved her Click'd kiosk sign, but she never even thought to save it. She certainly didn't ask anyone to autograph it.

She turned back to Nathan. "What did you want to show me?"

"That." Nathan pointed at a tall stack of boxes in the corner next to his closet.

Allie walked over to get a better look. Each box had a logo on one side. They were all from gaming companies. Clothing companies. Shoe companies. One of the bigger boxes had that telltale red-and-white Supreme logo on one side. "Is this the stuff from the sponsors?"

"Yep."

Nathan had told Allie all about the gifts when they first started arriving, but he hadn't mentioned anything in a while and she'd forgotten all about them.

For about a month or so after Games for Good, Nathan was a bit famous. He was interviewed on local TV stations and in the newspaper, and for two weeks solid, Built trended in the top spot on the Spyglass Games website. Companies started paying to sponsor billboards in his game, just like he hoped they would.

But eventually, he ran out of billboards, and he had to start a waiting list. That's when companies began sending him things, like shoes, clothes, and gaming equipment in hopes of improving their chances. Nathan hadn't even asked for any of it; the boxes just started showing up on his doorstep.

Allie had been jealous at the time. She hadn't been in any of the news coverage. No one had interviewed her. She didn't get a single surprise gift.

"Why is this all just sitting here?"

Nathan shrugged. "I don't know. I kept a lot of the clothes, but I really don't need the rest of this stuff. The shoes don't even fit me. It used to make me happy—but now, it . . . doesn't really."

Allie looked at him, realizing for the first time how much things had changed. She never stopped to consider how it must have felt when those packages stopped coming, or how it felt to be *someone*, until you suddenly weren't.

"I keep thinking I should sell it," Nathan said.

Allie began to realize where he was going with this. "Really?" she asked, eyes wide.

He squared his shoulders. "Don't get too excited. I'm not selling it all on Swap'd when I can make a small fortune selling it to total strangers online. But I figured it would be fun to sell one or two things. I thought you could help me decide."

Allie looked at him sideways. "Are you serious?"

He nodded.

She returned her attention to the stack, scanning up and down. If she owned two or three of those things, she would have been able to sell them and buy Courtney's plane ticket all by herself. She pushed the thought from her mind. Nathan was doing something nice for her. Something really, really nice.

"People seem to like those game controllers," she said. "There was a fierce battle for a Supreme sweatshirt today. I bet you could get a lot of money for that T-shirt or the beach towel. And I can name ten sneakerheads who will fight over those Adidas."

"Done." Nathan pulled one of the controller boxes from the stack, and then reached for one of the Adidas boxes. The stack wobbled like a Jenga game.

He tossed the two boxes onto his bed, and then brushed his hands together. "I'll post the controller tonight and the shoes tomorrow. I'll save the Supreme stuff for Monday . . . make all those hype beasts wait for it." He winked at her.

Allie stared at him. "Why are you doing this for me?"

He shrugged. "I don't know . . . Swap'd looks like fun. All this stuff is just sitting here. And, I guess, I could use the money."

"So, you're doing it for purely selfish reasons?"

"Why else would I do it?" Nathan folded his arms across his chest.

Allie raised an eyebrow.

"Okay, fine," Nathan said. "I'm not doing it for completely selfish reasons."

"No?"

"See, my computer science tablemate keeps going on and on about this friend of hers named Courtney." Nathan rolled his eyes. "It's so annoying. This Courtney person is *all* she ever talks about. Courtney this, and Courtney that. CodeGirls camp, and the Fishbowl, and gummy worms. Seriously, it makes it hard to concentrate."

Allie pressed her lips together, suppressing a grin. "Sounds horrible."

"It is. Trust me."

Allie looked at him. "Thank you."

He nodded. And then he held her gaze for a moment. "I saw what you did in the final auction." He spit the words out quickly, as if he'd been weighing whether or not he should say them.

"What do you mean?" Allie asked.

"The tutoring . . ."

She felt her face get hot. She tried to play it off. "I

know," she said. "It's silly, right? I need the money, and I'm running out of my own stuff to sell, so Zoe convinced me to sell tutoring sessions—"

"To SurfSup?" he asked, cutting her off.

"Well, that's who won, so . . . yeah."

"Because that's who you wanted to win."

Allie's stomach dropped. "I don't know what you're talking about."

"Sure you do. There were a few seconds left in the auction. And then . . ." He snapped his fingers. "There were zero."

Allie couldn't speak. Her chest felt tight. She wiped her palms on her jeans and tried to play it cool. *How did he know?*

"Hey, it's okay," Nathan continued. "You don't have to be embarrassed. And don't worry, your secret's safe with me."

But that wasn't the point. *He* knew she cheated. She wasn't embarrassed, she was mortified.

"So . . . who is he?" A playful grin tugged at the corners of his mouth. It was so kind, so disarming, Allie felt the heat begin to leave her cheeks.

"I can't tell you that. Everyone's a secret in Swap'd."

"But you like him."

The flush had barely left and it was already back again. "What makes you say that?"

"Because of the look on your face right now."

Allie scolded herself for being so transparent. "I

guess . . . I mean, I think so. Zoe says he's really nice, but I've barely talked to him. I trip over my tongue every time I try."

Nathan started cracking up. "You?"

"Yeah. Why?"

"It's just a little depressing, that's all. You're always so confident. If you can't talk to a guy, there is, like, zero chance I'll ever be able to talk to a girl."

"Oh, come on, you talk to me. I'm a girl."

"That doesn't count."

She put her hands on her hips. "How do I not count?"

"I didn't mean it like that. It's just . . . you're Allie. I've known you since kindergarten. You're my friend, so it's just . . . easy, I guess."

The words made Allie feel a little bit sad, but she wasn't sure why. They were true. And she felt the same way about him. Nathan was her friend. It was easy to talk to him. Everything about them was easy. If only she felt the same way around Marcus, she wouldn't have to sell tutoring sessions or cheat to make sure he won.

"So what are you going to leave in the locker for him tomorrow?"

Allie hadn't even thought about that part. "Do I have to leave him something?"

"What if he goes to the locker and there's nothing there?"

Nathan was right. And for $28, Marcus should probably

find *something* waiting for him. Something that told him that the next three days were going to be fun.

"I'll think of something," Allie said.

"Okay, but . . . how are you going to do the lessons when he can't know who you are?"

"By text and phone call." Allie told him all about her notebook she'd saved from the previous year, and then pulled out her phone and showed him the picture she'd taken earlier. "This is everything he'll be tested on."

Nathan looked over her shoulder while Allie translated the items on the list. "Apple, train schedule, wrench, balloon . . ."

"So, basic household stuff," Nathan said.

That gave Allie an idea. She turned to Nathan. "What if I leave these items in the locker, and then use them to teach the lessons?"

"I like it." He walked over to his desk and opened the top drawer. "Here, I'll get you started," he said, handing Allie a wrinkled train schedule.

She took it. And then she looked at the list again. "Got any apples?"

Nathan was already heading for the door. "Let's go check."

twenty-two

The fruit bowl in Nathan's kitchen was full. He grabbed a bright red apple off the top and tossed it to Allie. "What's next?"

She pointed at the cabinet where he'd gone for a glass when she first arrived. "Have a coffee mug?"

"Yep." He grabbed a black-and-orange San Francisco Giants mug off the second shelf and set it on the counter next to the apple.

Allie looked over the list again. "Wrench?"

"Follow me." They walked into the living room, through the laundry room, and out into the garage.

"Whoa," Allie said as the door closed behind her. It was

the cleanest garage Allie had ever seen. Half of the floor was painted white, but the other half was carpeted and filled with exercise equipment. The walls were lined with shelves and cabinets, and everything was labeled. It looked nothing like her garage, which looked, well, like a garage.

Nathan stepped up to a tall red tool cabinet and opened a drawer marked with the word "wrenches." "Take your pick," he said, stepping back so Allie could get a good view. She studied her choices, and then reached for the smallest one, figuring it was the least likely to be missed.

Nathan spun a slow three-sixty, scanning the shelves and cabinets for anything else on the list, and then came to a stop. "Didn't you need a shovel?" he asked, pointing at a shelf filled with gardening tools.

She dug around in the plastic bin until she found a small shovel with a blue handle. She took a step back and looked around Nathan's garage again. On the highest shelf, she spotted a plastic tub marked with the word "Camping."

"Think there's a flashlight in there?" she asked.

"Knowing my mom, there are probably a dozen of them."

Nathan grabbed a small ladder, and Allie steadied it while he climbed to the top, reached for the box, and carefully lowered it into Allie's hands. She set it on the ground, removed the cover, and searched inside, digging under the paper plates, extra utensils, bug spray, and campfire tools, until she found what she was looking for: a plastic bag filled with a bunch of small flashlights in various colors.

"Told you," Nathan said.

Allie took a green one out of the bag. She pressed the button to be sure it worked, and it cast a bright light on the wall. "Why do you have so many flashlights?"

"You always need flashlights when you're camping."

Allie shrugged as she clicked it off. "I wouldn't know. I've never been camping."

"What?" Nathan asked. "Never?"

"Yeah. Why? Is there something wrong with that?"

"There are so many things wrong with that, I don't even know where to start."

"Well, you can start by telling me why camping requires so many flashlights."

Nathan shook his head, like he couldn't believe he had to explain this. "Well, it's dark, and you need to be able to get around at night. My mom puts them all over the campsite and in the tents, so you can always find one." He reached into the bag, grabbed a red one, and flicked it on. "And, of course, you need them for ghost stories."

She stared at him. "What are you talking about?"

"Don't you like ghost stories?"

Allie nodded. "Of course I do. Emma, Maddie, Zoe, and I tell them every time we have a sleepover."

"And you don't know they're, like, ten times better with a flashlight?" He walked to the light switch, flicked it off, and then used the light to lead the way. When they reached the carpet, he stretched out, flat on his back, and patted the spot next to him. Allie settled in. "Okay," he said, "I'll go first."

He shined the light on the wooden beams above them. "Are you ready?" he whispered.

"I don't know," she whispered back. "I guess so."

He let the silence fill the room. And then, in a low, soft voice, he began. "A teenage girl was babysitting for a new family. Before the parents left, the mom told her that both kids had been having nightmares. She asked her to watch TV in the guest room after she put them to bed so she could hear them if they woke up."

He paused. Allie stared straight up at the ceiling, waiting for him to continue.

"Later that night, the babysitter put the kids to sleep," he said. "And then she went into the guest room, sat on the bed, turned on the TV, and started flipping through the channels. But she was having a hard time relaxing because of this creepy, life-size clown statue in the corner of the room.

"After a while, she couldn't take it anymore," Nathan continued. "She went downstairs and called the mom to ask if she could watch TV in the living room instead. The mom said that was fine, but then asked her why. The babysitter told her that the clown statue was creeping her out too much. There was silence on the other end of the line. And then the mom said, 'Go upstairs, get the children, and take them next door. Right now. I'll stay with you on the phone.' The babysitter did as she was told. When she was safely at the neighbor's, the mom calmly said, 'We don't have a clown statue.'"

After he delivered the last line, Nathan let out a loud, evil laugh as he brought his hand down slowly over the beam so it looked like a hand reaching down to grab them. Allie shrieked and jumped to her feet. Her heart was beating fast, but she couldn't stop giggling.

"See," Nathan said, cracking up. "So much better with a flashlight."

Allie covered her eyes.

"Okay, your turn."

Her heart was still racing as she settled back into her spot on the floor. He handed her the flashlight and she shined it straight up, like he had. Allie stayed still, letting the silence build tension before she began.

"It was late at night, and a couple was driving down a dark road when they noticed a young woman hitchhiking." Allie spoke slowly, keeping her voice low. "The couple decided to pull over, and the young woman climbed into the backseat. She thanked them and gave them an address that was only a mile away."

Allie kept the beam fixed on the ceiling, just like Nathan had.

"As they drove, the couple tried to make polite conversation, but the young woman didn't say a word. They reached the address and the driver stopped the car. He turned around. There was no one there. The couple had no idea what to do, so they agreed to go up to the house and knock on the door. An elderly woman greeted them, and they told her all about the young woman who had asked for a ride. 'She matches my daughter's description exactly,' the woman said. 'But . . . my daughter was killed in a car accident many years ago, almost exactly a mile up the road.' "

Allie let out a loud, maniacal laugh as she slowly lowered her hand over the beam. Nathan knew what to expect, of course, but that didn't stop him from shrieking in terror and curling up into a ball. That made Allie crack up.

When they were finally able to catch their breaths again, Nathan said, "Okay, what's next?"

"You want another ghost story? I have a bunch of them."

"I meant, what's next on your list?"

Allie looked at him, confused.

"SurfSup?"

"Right," she said, suddenly remembering the tutoring sessions with Marcus, and why they'd gone out to the garage in the first place. She pulled her phone from her pocket and held it up in the air so they could both see the screen.

"I think I can get the rest of these at home. Except this one." Her head fell to one side. "Where am I supposed to find a turtle?"

Nathan chuckled. "Yeah, I'm afraid I can't help you there."

He stood, and then reached down to help Allie up. "Thanks," she said.

She followed him into the kitchen. He brought the

dogs back inside, and then took a grocery bag from under the kitchen sink. "Here," he said, handing it to her.

She dropped in all the stuff they'd found in the garage and scooped everything off the counter. "Well, I guess I'm ready for my first lesson."

"I guess you are," Nathan said.

Back at home, Allie turned the bag upside down, dumping everything on her bed, and scanned the list again.

Un libro. A book. That was easy. She picked one of her favorite novels off her bookshelf and tossed it onto the bed.

Las gafas de sol. Sunglasses. She rifled through her desk drawer and unearthed a pair of white plastic frames with scratched lenses.

El champú. That was easy, too. Her mom always brought those little shampoo bottles home when she traveled for work. Allie walked to the bathroom and found what she needed right away.

Nothing left but *la tortuga.*

And then she realized she had that, too. The last time she'd cleaned her room, her mom had convinced her to donate all her old stuffed animals, but there were a few she couldn't stand to give away.

She opened her closet, reached up to the high shelf, and tugged at the pink canvas bin. She dug down deep, past the rabbits, and bears, and monkeys, until she found the stuffed turtle she used to carry around with her everywhere.

"Hey, Squirt." She kissed his nose and added him to the pile of stuff already on the bed.

And then she walked to her desk and found a bright blue note card in one of the drawers. In her best penmanship, she wrote:

Hi, Marcus!

She scratched it out.

She wasn't supposed to know who he was. And her writing looked too much like a girl's. Although with the name, Princess Peach, he'd probably figure that much. Still, she tore the card in half, tossed it into the trash can, and reached for another one. This time she tilted her hand a different way and wrote more slowly, making the letters look blockier and more nondescript.

Hey, SurfSup! I've never been a tutor, but

She stopped. "Ugh," she said, ripping the card in half. He didn't need to know that she'd never done anything like this before. She reached for another card

Hey, SurfSup! I'm your Spanish tutor. Let's get you an A on Tuesday's test! Can you meet tonight at 6:00 pm? Text me at 555-9588 to confirm.
— Princess Peach

Allie read it four times. And then she looked over at Bo. "Hey, buddy, listen to this." She read it aloud. "What do you think?"

Without opening his eyes, Bo rolled over on his side and tipped his head back, giving her easier access to the spot under his chin. Allie reached down and scratched it, as requested.

"I know, right? This is completely ridiculous."

She looked at everything strewn across her bed, thinking about how strange the last couple of hours had been. Nathan didn't have to do any of the things he'd done. He didn't have to sell his stuff, or help her collect things for Marcus, or tell stories by flashlight. He didn't have to keep her secret. He could have made her feel even worse about cheating at her own game, but he hadn't.

Allie dropped all the items back inside the bag, one by one. But when she reached the flashlight, she stopped. She turned it over in her hands a few times. And then she set it on her desk, went downstairs to grab a flashlight from the junk drawer, and returned, dropping it into the bag along with everything else. She added the note she'd written, stapled the bag across the top a few times, and wrote SURFSUP in thick black letters on the front.

friday

twenty-three

The bus arrived, the doors opened, and Allie climbed the steps, feeling brave, and bold, and on top of the world. She stopped at the landing, looked right at Marcus, and didn't wait for him to greet her first.

"Hey, Six," she said.

He looked taken aback, but then he sat up a little straighter and said, "Hey, Three."

Allie thought about all the items in her backpack. She couldn't wait to get to school and put them in the locker.

"Chat later, Ms. Navarro!" Mr. Steve yelled. "Seat. Now. Please."

Allie bounced to her seat and flopped down next to Zoe.

"Switching it up. I like that," Zoe said as she high-fived her. "See, my Marcus Plan is already working."

"It's a good day," Allie said. "And I have a feeling it's only going to get better."

Allie was right. All day, everywhere she went, everyone was talking about Swap'd.

She was sitting in math class, waiting for the bell to ring, when Evan leaned across the aisle and tapped Nick's shoulder to get his attention.

"Did you see today's auction?" he asked.

"Um . . . yeah," Nick said. "That gaming headset has to be worth a hundred bucks."

"Right? And the opening bid is forty bucks!" Evan added. "That thing is all mine."

"Ha! Good luck with that," Nick leaned back in his chair, folding his arms. "I'm going after it."

"So am I," Evan said, mimicking Nick's posture. "And I have sixty to spend."

"Good to know. It'll be easy to outbid you," Nick said, tipping his chin up. "My grandma was especially generous with birthday money this year."

It was like that in second, third, and fourth period, too. Allie couldn't help overhearing all the conversations about who was selling what, all the things people had planned to bid on, and how much they had to spend. They all whispered under their breaths, like they were part of a secret club.

Allie couldn't believe it was all happening. Her game was a success. This time, she'd done everything right. And she was going to keep it that way. She wasn't going to push the app beyond its limits. She wasn't going to get carried away, or get greedy, or get caught up in the popularity thing. And she wasn't going to fail. She was going to show Naomi Ryan that she deserved a spot in Hackathon. She still wasn't sure she'd take it, but she wanted to be picked. She wanted the chance to decide.

When the lunch bell rang, Allie found Emma, Maddie, and Zoe waiting at her locker again. Allie dialed the combination and lifted the latch. All four of them stood there, staring at the huge pile of money inside.

"Too bad you can't keep it all!" Emma added.

"Right? Ten percent seems like nothing," Allie said as she scooped all the bills into the big plastic bag she'd brought from home. "This is four hundred and forty-three bucks. If I could keep it, I'd be buying Courtney's plane ticket right now!" Allie zipped the bag closed and handed it to Emma, along with the list of winners. "You know what to do."

"On it," Emma said as she turned on her heel. Zoe and Maddie were right behind her, bee-lining for the library to divvy up the cash.

Allie raced to the eight-hundreds building and hid in her usual spot next to the garden, watching all the activity.

FlipFlop was there first. She dialed the combination, lifted the latch, and removed a bag of candy. A minute later, 3DPea arrived, opened the locker, and left holding her new sweatshirt. Spider-Pig took Chris's skateboard, ElevenWaffles grabbed her tub of blue slime, and SparkleMotion left with a fidget spinner and a bag of scrunchies.

And then Kelsey Gilbert stepped up, and Allie's heart started racing when she remembered what she'd done during the auction the day before. She felt sick to her stomach. But Kelsey didn't seem upset at all. She was smiling as she reached inside, pulled out one of Zoe's colorful bags full of candy and a new iPhone case.

Soon, a short line had formed, but everyone took it in stride. Each person stepped up and took their new purchase, and Allie checked each item off the list. It was all going to plan. There was only one problem: Marcus still hadn't arrived.

The bell rang, signaling that it was time to get to class.

Where was he? Had he changed his mind?

She'd be late for class if she stayed, but she couldn't leave—not now.

And then she spotted him walking toward locker #860 with long, purposeful strides. He stopped, dialed the combination, lifted the latch, grabbed the grocery bag, and took off again, right as the final bell rang.

Allie let herself breathe again as she checked his name off the list and then raced to the computer lab, hoping she could sneak in without anyone noticing. But when she opened the door, Ms. Slade was standing at the front of the room, leaning against her desk.

"You're late, Ms. Navarro."

"Sorry," Allie said, rushing to her computer station. "I was dealing with something on my project."

Ms. Slade returned to addressing the class. "I know you're all eager to get to work, but we're at the halfway point, so let's take a minute and check in on your projects first." She looked around the room. "Let's start with you, Ava. How's your geocaching game going?"

"Harder than I expected," Ava said. "I started beta testing it with a small group yesterday, but the coordinates were off on three of the locations. I think I fixed it at lunch today, so I'm going to go back out now and check the map."

"Good. How about you, Ben?"

"Pretty good," he said. "It's a virtual time capsule. People can add news clippings, music, YouTube videos, that kind of thing."

"And you'll be ready to roll out on Monday as planned?" Ms. Slade asked.

"Yep," he said. "I'll be ready."

"Sounds great. How about you in the back? How's everything going, Allie?"

"Great." She gave her an enthusiastic thumbs-up.

"Do you want to tell us what you're working on?"

Allie hesitated. Part of her wanted to tell Ms. Slade and the rest of the class about Swap'd. It would be fun to see the looks on their faces when she told them that her game had been up and running for three days already, that she had eighty-three users, and that she'd sold almost a thousand dollars' worth of stuff so far. But another part of her liked that it still felt kind of like a secret club; that it was all on the down-low. Nathan was the only person from advanced CS class that Allie had invited. Once the rest of them knew that Swap'd was her game, the whole school would know, too.

"Do I have to tell you?" she asked. "It's kind of a surprise."

Ms. Slade thought about it for a moment. "I guess not." She moved along. "How about you, Nathan?"

Nathan kicked his feet up onto the desk and leaned his chair back. "Mine's a surprise, too."

Ms. Slade looked like she might not let him off the hook, but she moved on to Jackson Barry anyway. When everyone's updates were complete, she sent them back to work. "If you need any help, you know where to find me."

Nathan pulled his headphones over his ears. And then he reached up, grabbed his monitor in both hands, and shifted it to the opposite edge of the desk so no one could see the screen, especially not Allie.

twenty-four

Swap'd

≡ **Swap'd** ⚙

All Auction Items

PopSocket - new!
Current bid: **$3**

Sweater - worn once!
Current bid: **$12**

Hoodie
Current bid: **$15**

Hacky Sack
Current bid: **$2**

Zoe slid into the seat next to Allie. "How's it lookin' today?"

"Good," Allie said without taking her eyes off her phone. "Sixty-seven players logged in. Two minutes till start time."

The queue looked good, too. There was a lot more variety than there was the day before—more clothes, more games, more phone cases, more jewelry, and even more fidget spinners. There were sneakers, stickers, baseball cards, board games, Hacky Sacks, stuffed animals, and PopSockets. And people were starting to get creative. One sixth grader named ProperPrim was offering to braid hair in the quad during lunch, and, for the right price, an eighth grader named CheesyPoofs would serve detention in your place.

The clock hit three thirty and the auction began.

This auction was different than the others. There were a lot more players, but most of them were new to the game, and they were only lurking. The same people were actively playing, but they were going after specific things, and quickly dropping out when the prices got too high.

Allie watched each auction, mentally totaling up her take each time. By three forty-five, she'd only made $8. By three fifty, she was up to $10. The items were getting cheaper, starting lower, and not being bid on as aggressively. As the clock ticked on, the game ran out of steam.

But then, the fourth auction began, and Nathan's gaming headset was up. He started the bidding at $40.

There weren't many other big-ticket items in that round, so it had everyone's attention.

Allie and Zoe bent over Allie's screen, silently rooting him on.

Sundawg jumped in first, raising the $40 starting bid straight to $45, and that was all it took. The whole place went nuts. Spider-Pig raised it to $46, ScrappyDoo raised it to $47, and Buh-Buy raised it straight to $50.

And that's when the outbursts began. Someone yelled,

"This is insane!" and another girl two rows in front of Allie slapped her hand hard against the window.

Some guy at the front of the bus stood up and yelled, "Oh, ScrappyDoo . . . you're toast, man!" And a guy at the back of the bus yelled, "Get him, Alex!"

Apparently, that was all Alex needed to hear. He lifted his phone in the air and yelled, "Watch me!"

LastPopTart jumped in and raised it to $57.

"If I have to pull over again, you all have detention!" Mr. Steve yelled.

The bus quieted down, but not for long. When ScrappyDoo pulled into the lead with a $62 bid, everyone went crazy again.

"Keep going," Allie whispered.

She wanted more.

And she knew Nathan wanted more.

And she knew they had it to spend.

As soon as the clock hit the ten-second mark, everything kicked into a whole new gear, and in a matter of seconds, the headset was up to $65.

Three.

Two.

One.

LuckyCharms bid $68 and *cha-ching!* The auction ended. The leaderboard appeared, shuffling everyone around, knocking SweetTooth down to #3, adding BooBooBear to #2, and sliding RiskItBiscuit into the #1 spot.

"Yes!" Zoe screamed, happy to still have a top position.

The system automatically sent out a message announcing the winner of each item and followed them up with the usual instructions for the sellers and buyers. And then it kicked out a message to everyone:

THANKS FOR SWAP'N!
NEXT AUCTION ON MONDAY AT 3:30 P.M.!

Thanks to Nathan's headset, Allie made a total of $25.

It was good, but not good enough. She hoped Courtney had a much better day.

She hugged Zoe and raced for the bus doors.

"See ya, Six," she said to Marcus as she rounded the corner.

But she didn't even hear him reply. She was already off the bus, sprinting across her lawn, and dialing Courtney at the same time. Courtney answered on the first ring.

"How did you do?" Allie asked as she dug in her backpack for her keys.

"Not good," Courtney said. "I'm all out of my own stuff, so I only brought in fourteen dollars. How about you?"

Allie opened the door, dropped her things in the entryway, and crouched down to let Bo cover her cheeks with kisses while she delivered the bad news. "I only made twenty-five."

"We're forty-eight dollars short," Courtney said.

"We'll get it on Monday, for sure!" Allie said, trying to look on the bright side.

Courtney was silent for a long time. "Yeah," she finally said, forcing a smile. "Monday."

twenty-five

At 6:00 p.m. on the dot, Allie typed her message:

Allie

¡Hola, SurfSup!

He replied right away.

Marcus

Who is this?

Allie

Princess Peach

Marcus

I was kidding

Allie froze. She didn't know what to say to that.

Sort of . . .

I don't get to know
who you really are?

You bought *anonymous*
tutoring sessions

I thought I was the
anonymous one

You are. And so am I ;)

Marcus

Tell me one thing about you.
Do we have any classes together?

She didn't want to tell him the truth. That would narrow it down too much. But she didn't want to lie to him, either.

Allie

Maybe

Do you ride my bus?

Maybe

Do you play a sport?

There was only one way to reply.

Maybe

Let's get going with our lesson

She started typing fast, hitting SEND before he had a chance to ask any more questions that might give her away.

Allie

> First, let me explain how this works

> 1: I will speak in English but you can only reply in Spanish

> 2: You can't google the answers. If you don't know, tell me you don't know

> BTW, "I don't know" in Spanish is "no lo sé"

> 3: For today, you can use your notes, but after that, no notes

> That's it. Any questions?

Marcus

Yeah

Will I ever know who you are?

"Nope," Allie said. But she typed something else.

Allie

> Maybe

She moved along as quickly as she could.

> Did you get the bag of stuff?

She already knew he had. She'd watched him pick it up.

Marcus

Yeah

> Good. Show me el horario del tren

A few seconds later, Marcus replied with a picture of the wrinkled train schedule Nathan had pulled from his desk drawer the day before. She pictured that look of satisfaction on Nathan's face as he handed it to her. "What's next?" he'd asked excitedly, like the two of them were partners in a scavenger hunt and they were determined to win.

> Good. Now show me la manzana

Marcus was even faster this time. In the picture he sent, he was holding it up to his chest. It was hard not to notice his chest. And his shoulders. She could tell he was wearing the same Mercer Mustangs T-shirt he'd worn to school that day. Too adorable.

> Bueno. Now show me la llave

At first, Marcus replied with a picture of him holding up the garden shovel, but when Allie told him that was incorrect, he got the wrench right on the next try.

> Show me una linterna

Marcus held the flashlight at his chin so the beam blocked his face, and Allie couldn't help but laugh. But then she felt a strange lump in her throat, and she didn't know why.

Marcus

You there?

> Yeah. Good

Allie looked through her notes, reminding herself what she'd planned to do next.

> Now without cheating, I want you to use each one of the items in a sentence. Any sentence you want

Marcus

En español?

> Sí

Ok...

The ellipses made him sound hesitant.

> Don't worry. I'll help you if you need it

Allie waited for a while. Finally, he replied.

Marcus

Disculpe, ¿puede indicarme la tren estación?

It was close. He got the structure a little bit backward, but it was easy to fix. Allie explained, then asked him for another sentence.

At seven o'clock, Allie's alarm signaled the end of their session. Allie let out a sigh of relief, and that surprised her. She had expected to be sad when it was over, but she wasn't. The whole thing felt like work. Maybe it was all totally normal. Allie wasn't sure.

Allie

That's it for tonight

Can we meet again on Sunday?

Why not tomorrow?

She couldn't tell him she had a soccer tournament all day; that would give her away. But she didn't want to lie to him, either.

> I can't. I'm booked

She left it at that. Let him think she had other tutoring clients. Let him think she wasn't as excited about their next meeting as she actually was.

> Keep practicing

> We'll pick up where we left off

> Sunday at 6

She wasn't about to tell him who she was, but she signed off with a little hint: the words he'd been hearing her say every day for the last four months, but with a little twist.

> See ya, SurfSup

She was pretty sure he knew who she was when he replied.

Marcus

> See ya, Peach

saturday

twenty-six

"Emma!" Allie yelled, waving her arms in the air.

Emma looked over her right shoulder, saw that Allie was open, and passed her the ball. Allie took it, dribbling down the field, dodging green jerseys, heading straight for the goal.

She was almost there when she spotted Maddie darting out from behind another defender. Allie didn't have to kick it very hard for it to skim across the grass and stop right in front of her.

Maddie moved the ball down the field, in total control as she dodged another defender.

"You got it, Maddie!" Allie yelled.

Maddie lined herself up and kicked it as hard as she could. The ball soared right past the goalie's hip and slammed into the back of the net.

Maddie took two steps backward. The horn sounded, signaling the end of the game. Final score: 3–2. "Yes!" she screamed, punching her fist into the air.

Allie and Emma were there within seconds, wrapping their arms around her shoulders and hugging her so hard, they lifted her feet off the ground.

The tournament was almost over. Three games down, one more to go, and a two-hour break in between.

The girls collected their things and walked to the sidelines, where their parents were standing in a big circle, trying to decide where to go for lunch. Allie didn't care; she just couldn't wait to sit down and throw back the biggest glass of ice water in existence.

Finally, everyone agreed on the deli at the shopping center across the street. The parents started walking. The girls trailed behind.

"Okay," Emma said as she grabbed Allie's hand. "Tell us all about the tutoring session with Marcus last night.

"I told you already!" Allie said.

"Over group text," Maddie said. "That doesn't count."

"Details," Zoe said. "Spill it."

As they walked, Allie told them all about the list of items, and the bag of stuff she and Nathan had collected for Marcus to pick up at the locker the day before. She told them how cute he sounded, even over text.

They arrived at the deli. They were all about to step inside when Emma stopped and said, "You guys . . . look."

Allie, Maddie, and Zoe followed her gaze.

Right next to the restaurant was a huge store with a big green sign that read EVERYTHING'S A DOLLAR.

"I need more glitter," Emma said.

"I need candy," Zoe said.

"I need cute wrapping paper," Maddie said.

Allie thought about the remaining items on her Marcus list. She still needed a few things she hadn't been able to find around the house, like a balloon and a birthday candle. "I need a few things for Marcus."

"Aw . . ." Emma grabbed Allie's arm.

"That's so cute!" Maddie bumped her shoulder against Allie's. "Soon you two are going to be all cute and *couple-y*, like Chris and me. The four of us can go to the movies together."

"Yeah," Allie said.

She tried to picture going to the movies with Marcus. Or holding hands with him in the hallway, like Chris and Maddie did. She couldn't see it clearly. The flirting thing was fun, but she'd never really thought about what happened after that.

"I'll tell our parents we're making a stop," Zoe said as she peeled off from the group. "Meet you there."

The rest of them walked through the automatic doors, grabbed a plastic basket from the stack, and looked around, trying to figure out where to go first.

"This place is gigantic," Maddie said.

They all stood there, feet rooted in place, waiting for someone to make the first move.

"I wonder where the birthday section is?" Allie asked.

They were about to head off to find it, when Zoe stepped in front of them, basket in hand, and said, "Follow me!"

She led them to the center of the store, where a massive aisle of candy seemed to stretch on forever. Zoe seem unfazed as she began reaching into the bins.

"I've made forty bucks, and that's what I'm spending," she said as she grabbed ten boxes of twenty-count Snickers bars, ten more boxes of Milky Ways, five boxes of Twix, and five more boxes of Three Musketeers. And then she started filling her basket with bags of Starbursts, Skittles, and Jolly Ranchers.

"That's a *lot* of candy," Emma said.

Zoe shrugged. "It's a dirty job, but someone's got to do it."

"Okay, my turn," Maddie said, waving everyone over to the wrapping-paper section. "It's all about the presentation," she said as they arrived at the aisle full of colorful paper tubes, buckets of bows, and rolls of ribbon. "Give it a few days, and word will get around that when you buy from Fashionista, it's a lovely experience, beginning to end." She scrunched up her nose. "Unlike CrabbyPatty, who delivers her clothes wrinkled and doesn't even bother to fold them first."

Maddie reached for a tube of white paper with bright orange flowers. "What about this? Too flowery?" Maddie didn't wait for her friends to respond. "No, it's perfect. It says fun *and* classy, don't you think?" She grabbed a roll of orange ribbon to match and carefully selected five white bows.

"I like this idea. I'm going to make my candy bags cuter, too." Zoe looked down, considering her options. She decided on cellophane gift bags with pictures of colorful assorted fruits. "See, this is festive. Strawberries. Cherries. Blueberries. Peaches. It'll make people feel like they're eating something healthy—"

"Unlike this." Emma picked up one of the Three Musketeer bags. "What is nougat even made of?"

"Magic," Zoe said. She took it from Emma's hand and tossed it back into her basket. "I'm going to fill these little bags with three dollars' worth of candy and sell them for ten. By this time next week, I'm going to be rolling in cash. *Roll-ing*, people!"

"Okay, my turn," Emma said as she led everyone over to the crafts section. She added purple, gold, and green glitter to her basket, along with a big container of Elmer's Glue. Then she stopped and looked around. "I need to find something to put all my slime in."

Everyone followed Emma to the kitchen section and peeled off down different aisles, looking for storage containers. Zoe found some glass jars with cute lids, and Emma put ten in her basket.

"What do you need, Allie?" Maddie asked.

Allie looked at the picture she'd taken on her phone. "A balloon. A candle." She shook her head. "I don't even know how I'm supposed to get all this stuff to him before our next tutoring session tomorrow."

"We'll deal with that later," Maddie said. "First, let's get the stuff you need. This way." They ran around the store, gathering up the small list of items, until they were down to the last one.

"A chair." Allie looked at her friends. "How am I supposed to give him a chair?"

They were all quiet for a minute. And then Zoe's head snapped up. "My little sister has a dollhouse! Come over after the game. You can all spend the night. We'll make slime together, fill the candy bags, and wrap Maddie's clothes."

Allie pictured them in a circle on Zoe's bedroom floor, working together on their auction items for Monday. And then she had an idea.

"Marcus only lives a few blocks away," Allie said. "We can sneak over after it gets dark and drop the bag at his house. I'll be right back!" Before her friends could say anything, she took off for the wrapping-paper aisle. She picked out a red gift bag and a colorful bow and returned to the register.

"For Marcus," she said, playing with the bow. "I figured he deserved something better than a plain old grocery bag."

■ ■ ■

Later that night, Zoe and Allie left Maddie and Emma watching a movie and slipped away to deliver the bag. They grabbed their jackets off the coat rack, lifted the hoods over their heads, and slid out the front door. Two blocks later, Zoe stopped behind a tall hedge. "That's it," she said.

Allie looked up. It was one of those old Victorian houses, with blue shingles, white trim, and a big turret window on one side. She peered around the shrub, checking to be sure they were alone out there, and gathering her nerve. Before she had time to overthink it, she stepped into the walkway, climbed the front stairs, set the bag down in front of the door, and ran back to her hiding place.

Her fingers were trembling as she typed.

Allie

Check your porch

They waited. A minute later, they heard the dead bolt unlock and the door open. Zoe squeezed Allie's hand. And then they heard the door close again.

"Let's go." Allie tightened her jacket around her waist, and they started walking back to Zoe's house. But right before they turned the corner, she slowed her steps and stole a glance over her shoulder.

Marcus was standing at his window with his hands cupped to the glass.

"Shoot!" Allie pulled her hood around her head. "He just saw us!"

Zoe started to turn around to look for herself, but Allie grabbed her arm and pulled her out of sight.

"Even if he did, he couldn't tell who you were," Zoe said. "It's too dark out here."

Allie hoped she was right.

sunday

twenty-seven

Allie checked the clock above the kitchen sink.

"Do you have somewhere you need to be?" her dad asked.

"Me? No. Why?" She stole another glance at the time.

"Because you keep checking the clock," he said.

"And you're not eating," her mom added.

"I'm eating." Allie stabbed her fork into a piece of chicken, popped it into her mouth, and forced it down. She didn't have room in her stomach for food—not with all those annoying butterflies.

Her dad returned to the story he'd been telling, and Allie returned to her dinner, but it was impossible to eat when her legs were jittery, and her heart was racing, and she couldn't stop shifting in place.

"What is with you tonight?" her mom asked.

"Big test." It wasn't a total lie. *She* didn't have a big test, but Marcus did. "May I be excused?"

"Not until you eat something."

Allie stabbed a bite of chicken and waited until her dad started talking again. Then she lowered the fork to her side and held it there, letting Bo clean it. She gave him another, and another. She checked the clock again. Ten minutes to go.

"Now may I be excused?"

Her mom checked her plate and said, "Fine."

"Come on, Bo," she called, and the two of them raced up the stairs.

She paced her room. She studied her notes. She rehearsed what she was going to say. And at 6:00 p.m., she typed:

Allie

¡Hola!

Marcus

¡Hola!

Are you ready for lesson #2?

Let's go

He sent a photo of all the items, the ones they'd studied on Friday night, mixed in with all the new stuff she and Zoe had delivered the night before. It was so strange to see all those things that belonged to Nathan, Zoe, and her, just lying on Marcus's bedroom rug.

Let's start with the items
we worked on last Friday

They flew through the first ten the same way they had before. But Marcus was much faster that time. And then they moved on to the second ones.

El helado

Allie thought back to the night before, when she and her friends sat on the floor in Emma's bedroom, passing around the carton of ice cream so they could help her empty it.

A minute later, her phone chirped, and up popped a picture of Marcus, hiding behind the empty mint chip container. Allie laughed.

Allie

> Excelenté. Now show me la silla

Marcus replied with a selfie of him from the forehead up, the tiny dining room chair perched on top of his head. Allie smiled. Zoe's little sister had demanded an entire tub of slime as payment for letting her borrow it.

> Now show me el globo

Allie started cracking up when she saw the picture. He'd blown up the purple balloon and used it to block his face.

The two of them went through all the items three times, until it was clear Marcus knew them cold. Then she asked him to use each one in a sentence. Like before, he was faster than she'd expected.

Allie had been hoping to put off pronunciation until

the final lesson, but they still had twenty minutes left and there was nothing else to do. She had no choice. It was time.

Allie

> **I think you're ready to work on pronunciation**

Marcus

How?

> **I'll call you**

Her stomach started doing these uncomfortable flip-flops as she dialed his number. He answered on the first ring.

"Hey." Allie made her voice lower. She thought it would make her sound more serious, but it made her feel ridiculous.

"Hey." The phone was silent. "So . . . how am I doing?"

"Great!" Allie said nervously. "Really great."

"Yeah?"

"Yeah. You've got this."

More silence. Allie shifted in her chair, trying to think of something to say. But Marcus beat her to it. "So," he said. "Are you going to tell me who you are now?"

"Nope."

"Well, clearly you know who I am, since you know where I live."

Allie hadn't thought about that part. "True," she said.

"It's okay. You don't have to tell me," he said. "I think I've already figured it out from the clues."

She let out a shaky breath. "What clues?"

"Like . . . I know you've been to Hawaii."

Allie had never been to Hawaii. "How do you know that?"

"The shampoo bottle is from the Kona Hilton."

The bottle she'd taken from her mom's bathroom drawer must have been from her business trip last summer. "Interesting."

"I thought I knew where you lived because of the train schedule, but now I'm stumped."

"What do you mean?"

"There's a map with a little circle around the corner of Twenty-First and California. I thought that was where you lived, but then, last night, you dropped off the stuff on my doorstep. So I figure you must live within walking distance. . . ." He paused, waiting for her to say something, but Allie didn't reply.

The whole thing was getting way too dicey.

"Okay, so now we're going to practice pronunciation and conversation," Allie said, shaking off their previous topic. "Like before, I want you to come up with a sentence using each of the twenty items, but this time, you have to say it, okay? And remember, if you don't know what to do, just say, '*No lo sé.*'"

Marcus didn't speak right away. She wondered if he was going to go back to guessing her identity. But then she heard the sound of paper shuffling in the background, and she realized he was trying to come up with a sentence.

"*¿Te gusta el pastel de manzana?*"

He said the words slowly, and a little awkwardly, but he got everything in the right order. "That was really good." She helped him with the pronunciation on *manzana*, and then said, "Okay, next—"

He cut her off. "Wait a second . . . You have to answer my question. You said we were working on pronunciation *and* conversation, didn't you?"

He was right. And it reminded her of what Zoe had said on the bus the week before. This was why Allie had auctioned off tutoring sessions in the first place: to have a real conversation with Marcus Inouye.

"Yes, I like apple pie," she said. And then she got right back to business. "Next sentence. Take your time."

Marcus kept going, creating sentences from each of the twenty items. Allie helped him along the way. He finished all twenty sentences just a minute before their time was up.

"Is there anything else you want to work on tonight?" Allie asked.

She was waiting for him to answer, when her mom knocked at the door. "Allie! Come down and empty the dishwasher." She covered the phone and hoped Marcus hadn't heard her, but it didn't matter, because now Bo was barking at the door.

"Quiet, Bo!" And then she cupped her hand over her mouth.

"Bo, huh?" Marcus asked. Allie squeezed her eyelids shut. "Another clue."

"So I have a dog," Allie said. "Everyone has a dog."

"Not me," he said. "I can't stand them."

Allie forgot all about her slipup and zeroed in on this new information. "You don't like *dogs?*"

"I got bit when I was little. They've terrified me ever since."

"Well, you've never met Bo. He's the cutest, sweetest, most adorable dog in the world. He'd never hurt anyone." She reached down to pet him, and he rolled over to one side so she could rub his tummy.

"I've met adorable dogs before. I still don't like them."

The alarm went off, and Allie pushed her disbelieving thoughts aside. "Time's up," she said.

Marcus was quiet on the other line. "Hey," he began. "I've been thinking . . . maybe we should meet in person for our last lesson. You already know who I am. Shouldn't I know who you are?"

But then I'd have to see you, Allie thought. *And talk to you. In person.* She cringed at the idea alone.

"Besides . . ." he continued. "I think I already know who you are."

"Do you?"

"I saw you the other night."

"Oh," she said.

"Oh," he echoed. She could hear the smiley-sounding lilt in his voice. Allie waited for him to say her name. He didn't. Instead he said, "So . . . tomorrow? In the library after school?"

He knew who she was. He knew, and he wanted to meet her in person. She couldn't wait to tell Zoe that her Marcus Plan had worked. It actually worked!

"Sure. Why not," Allie said. She hoped she sounded cool. "Bring all twenty items with you."

"Okay . . ."

He didn't hang up. She was still waiting for him to say her name. She was dying to say his.

"See you, Princess Peach."

"See you, SurfSup."

They hung up.

Allie squealed, dancing around her room. She couldn't wait to call Zoe and tell her everything. She was about to dial her number when her phone chirped.

Courtney

CALL ME!

BAD NEWS!

twenty-eight

Courtney answered the FaceTime call on the first ring. "The ticket just went up to four hundred and twenty-five dollars! What are we going to do?"

Allie let out a breath. "That's it? It's no big deal," she said.

"No big deal? How can you say that? We only needed forty-eight bucks. Now we need seventy-three!"

"I'll make that much all on my own. Look at my queue." Allie waited while Courtney switched over to the right screen. "I'm selling the DS. There are four really good video games. There's a pair of Air Force Ones, and Nathan posted the Adidas and a bunch of Supreme gear—all the stuff that people fight over. Someone's even selling a monitor."

"How are you going to deliver that?"

"I have no idea!" Allie giggled. "But I'll figure it out."

"You have a lot more than I do," Courtney said.

"I know! Everyone's totally into it."

"And you're definitely selling the DS this time?" Courtney asked.

Allie held it up to the screen and did a little dance in place. "Number three is Dry Bones," she sang. "And I have the rest of the night to unlock number four."

"Can I just tell you who it is? You have to sell it—"

Allie cut her off. "I will, no matter what. Look, I already posted it." She had taken her time photographing the DS from all different angles. She'd even spread all the games across her bedroom floor to make it look more impressive. "I started the bidding at forty."

"You'll get at least that." Courtney got quiet and Allie could tell she was estimating everything. "Okay," she finally said, letting out a heavy sigh. "I think we can do it, but this one's up to you. I've got a bunch of lower-priced stuff, and I'm all out of my own things to sell. At ten percent, I'll be lucky if I pull in twenty bucks."

Allie brought the phone close to her face. "We've got this. I promise. By this time tomorrow, we'll have your plane ticket in hand."

Courtney's face relaxed. "You're sure?"

"I'm *positive.*" Allie said it with all the certainty she felt.

She pictured herself standing in front of Naomi Ryan on Saturday, demonstrating Swap'd, telling them how it went from idea to working game in less than twenty-four hours. For the hundredth time, she thought about the Hackathon application, just waiting for her to press SEND.

She almost told Courtney. She wanted to. But then Courtney jumped to her feet, looking more elated than she had in days, and let out an optimistic cheer. "In that case, I'm going to stop worrying and go straight to celebrating!"

"Achievement unlocked dance party?" Allie asked instead.

"You read my mind!"

It was a Fishbowl tradition. Anytime someone hit a huge milestone, their teacher cranked up the music, and they all danced around the lab. Allie picked a song, pressed play, and climbed on top of her bed. Courtney did the same. They started jumping, making faces at each other each time they were airborne.

"In five days, we'll both be jumping on this bed!" Allie screamed. "Because you'll be here in San Francisco!"

"Five days!"

"Five sleeps!"

"We're going to Game On!" Courtney screamed back. Then she stopped jumping. "Allie!"

Allie stopped jumping, too. "What?"

They were both beaming, and sweating, and panting, trying to catch their breaths.

"We did it. We actually did it!"

"Of course we did. Why would you ever doubt *us*?"

"It will never happen again."

Allie held her pinky finger up to the screen. "Pinkie swear?"

Courtney pressed hers against the glass. "Pinkie swear."

monday

twenty-nine

"I was *this* close to getting that gaming head-set," Evan said.

"I was even closer," Nick said.

"Wait, so you're not LuckyCharms?" Evan asked.

"I wish," Nick said. "I had that thing locked in, and then at the last second, he swooped in and outbid me!"

She, Allie thought, grinning to herself. If the two of them only knew they'd lost to Cassie Finn, a girl, and a *sixth* grader at that.

Allie had been impressed with Cassie's strategy. She'd been logged in the whole time, watching the auction for almost the full five minutes before she finally made one single death blow of a move. Evan and the rest of them hadn't even seen her coming.

"That was a steal. I can't believe it only went for sixty bucks. Those things are a hundred bucks, easy."

Allie had never been so happy to be anonymous. Everywhere she went, she overheard people talking about the upcoming auction. They talked about it in the bathroom, during passing periods, and during every one of her classes. This time, she wasn't the game's creator—she was one of them.

A few people had started to make the connection to Click'd, though. Cory Johannsen stopped her in the hall to ask if Swap'd was her game, but she just shrugged and said, "Maybe." In PE, Avery Duncan caught up to her on the track and casually said, "So . . . Swap'd, huh?" Allie grinned at her and said, "Isn't it fun?" And then she took off at a sprint.

It was only a matter of time before word got out. Eventually, someone would see her taking cash out of her locker or spot her checking the status of the pickups. And that was fine. When it happened, she'd own it proudly. For now, Allie was having too much fun being exactly like everyone else.

When the lunch bell rang, Allie launched into action. She met Emma at her locker and handed her the money. She counted out Nathan's take and stuffed it into a plain white envelope. She couldn't wait to get to the computer lab, to deliver it personally.

She ran off to the eight-hundreds building, hid behind the student garden, and watched everyone pick up the things they'd bought on Friday. All throughout lunch, people kept walking up to the locker, removing PopSockets and Hacky Sacks, iPhone cases and bath bombs, nail polish and video games, bags of candy and tubs of slime.

When the locker was empty, Allie checked the time. There were ten more minutes left before lunch ended. Her friends had all the payment deliveries under control. She'd checked the queue for that afternoon's auction more times than she could count. She had nothing else to do, so she headed to the lab early.

Ms. Slade looked up from her desk when Allie stepped inside. "I was wondering if you were going to stop by."

Allie was surprised to see the lab empty. On release day it was usually packed with people, scrambling to finish their projects. "Where is everyone?"

"Oh, they've been here. It's been a busy lunch. In fact, you and Nathan are the only ones I haven't seen."

Allie played it cool, but inside, she felt like she was about to burst. She liked hearing that the rest of her classmates were rushing to finalize their games while she'd had hers up and running for almost a week.

She walked to her workstation.

"How about giving me a little look?" Ms. Slade asked, following her. "You've been working so hard all week and I have no idea what you've been building back here. I can't wait to see what my star student has created this time."

Allie's whole body felt lighter. She'd never really thought of herself as Ms. Slade's star student. Wasn't that Nathan? He was the one who made her so proud during Games for Good. He was the one who won every coding competition and science fair since the third grade. Allie wasn't sure what she had done to deserve that title, but she liked the sound of it.

She sat up taller in her chair and brought her fingers to the keyboard. "Sit down," she said proudly. "I'll give you a demo."

She typed in her password, navigated over to the server, and turned the monitor so Ms. Slade could see the screen.

"You always tell us to look around, to get ideas from the real world . . . to notice the way people already do things and look for ways technology can help improve them, right? Well, that's what I did. Kids buy and sell things here on campus all the time—stuff like video games, controllers, clothes . . . all kinds of stuff. So it got me thinking, why not make a game out of it? What if people could sell their stuff, make money, and compete with each other all at the same time?"

Allie started with the backend code, explained how it worked at a high level, and how they'd built it so quickly. "I used my leaderboard code from Click'd, but every-thing else—the auction engine, the interface, the avatar creator—all came from my CodeGirls summer camp friends. You were right. We snapped everything together, connected it with some new code, and that was it. We had a completely new app."

Allie was reaching for her phone, preparing to click on the icon and demo the app itself, when Ms. Slade said, "Hold on." She leaned in closer, resting her elbows on her knees.

Something wasn't right. Allie could tell from her voice. "What?" she asked.

"Allie," Ms. Slade said carefully. "I love this idea. I really do. But I'm afraid it won't work."

Allie couldn't wait to tell her she was wrong; it *was* working. It was working *perfectly*.

"Selling items on campus is not only against school rules, it's against the law," Ms. Slade said.

Allie stared at her. "What do you mean, against the law? It happens all the time."

"I'm sure it does, but it's not supposed to. California law says you can't sell *anything* within one thousand feet of school property. It might seem unfair, but the law is designed to keep you safe while you're at school."

"But still—" Allie began.

Ms. Slade cut her off. "I can't condone this. I could get in trouble, too."

Allie had no idea what to say. No idea what to do. A week's worth of work, a queue full-to-bursting with products to sell, and Courtney's plane ticket on the line. This couldn't be right.

Ms. Slade scooted her chair in closer. "Hey, it's okay. You've done great work here. I love how you embraced the assignment and pulled in code from all your friends. That's exactly what I was looking for."

Allie wanted to scream.

Ms. Slade's eyes lit up. "Here's an idea: You can't roll this out across campus, but maybe we can find a way to play it with a smaller group of students. Why don't you deploy it the class? We can do, like, a mock auction, you know? We can all pretend to buy and sell stuff." She picked up Allie's mouse and dangled it in the air. "Who knows, maybe you'll sell this for a thousand dollars. That would be fun."

It was all Allie could do to sit there and not bolt for the door. "Yeah," she said under her breath. "Fun."

"Well, I know you, and I know you'll come up with something." She stood and brushed her hands on her jeans. "You definitely aced the reuse assignment. Whatever you decide to do next doesn't matter. I'm already impressed."

Allie felt sick. As Ms. Slade turned and walked back to her desk, Allie switched over to the screen she hadn't shown Ms. Slade: The queue, filled with more items than ever before, all estimated to sell for more than five hundred dollars.

thirty

"Are you sure you're okay?" Nathan asked again.

"Are you sure you're okay?" Nathan asked again.

Allie nodded without looking at him. Just as she'd done the last four times he asked her that question.

"I can tell something's wrong. Why won't you tell me?"

She couldn't, because if she told him, that would make it real. And if she made it real, she'd think of Courtney, and then she'd fall apart. And she wasn't about to let that happen, not in front of her entire class, and certainly not in front of Nathan.

Nathan.

When he found out, he'd be nice and understanding, but deep down, she knew what he'd really be feeling: pity.

She didn't want his pity—she'd had plenty of that last fall when Click'd failed miserably, and oh-so publicly. She wanted his respect. She wanted Ms. Slade's respect, and Naomi Ryan's respect, and the class's respect, and the whole school's respect. She wanted to *wow* them all.

She barely had time to enjoy her status as Ms. Slade's star student, and it was already coming to a screeching halt.

"You sure you're okay?" Nathan asked again.

"I'm fine."

She wished he'd quit asking. Every time he did, she wanted to scream. Until the last ten minutes, he knew everything about her game, and she knew nothing about his. Now she knew one thing: He was going to beat her. Again.

"Why won't you talk to me?"

Allie couldn't bite her tongue a second longer. She turned to him, hands shaking, blood boiling. "Why won't I talk to *you*? I have. I've told you everything. You're the one who won't talk to *me*. You're the one with all the secrets and the surprises," she said, wiggling her fingers and rolling her eyes sarcastically. "Why won't you tell me what you're working on, Nathan?"

"Because I can't."

"Why not? Because you don't even consider me your competition anymore?"

"No . . . that's not it."

Allie fixed her gaze on his. "That *is* it, isn't it? You're too good for all of this?" A few kids at the closest workstations turned around in their chairs to see what was going on, so she lowered her voice. "You've got this assignment in the bag. And I bet you already got into the hackathon program, too, didn't you? That's why you don't seem at all concerned about any of this. That's why it's all a big secret."

"You have no idea what you're talking about!" Nathan said, raising his voice. "And you're one to talk. Last time I checked, you had a huge secret that only I know about."

Allie glared at him, teeth clenched, hands balled into fists by her side. She hated that Nathan knew she'd cheated. She should have known he'd hold it over her head at some point.

"Actually," Nathan continued, "you don't have one secret, you have two!"

"No, I don't."

"Oh, yeah? When are you planning to tell Courtney that you're applying to Hackathon?"

Allie didn't reply. She couldn't.

"See," he said slowly. "I'm not the only one with secrets, Allie."

The truth in his words hit her hard. Her chest felt tight and she could feel tears begin to sting her eyes. He was right. She did have secrets. But hers weren't the same. Not at all.

She forced in a deep breath and squared her shoulders. "I might be keeping secrets, Nathan, but mine are different."

"Oh, really? How?"

Allie stood. "I'm not keeping them from you."

She needed to get out of there. Fast. But she could barely move and hold the tears back at the same time. She finally made it to Ms. Slade's desk and asked for the bathroom pass.

She waited until she was alone in the hallway to let the tears fall.

That hollow, empty feeling in her chest was too familiar. It was exactly how she felt during Games for Good, watching those nine kids unveil their games on stage while she sat in the audience and watched. How could this be happening again?

She'd created an amazing app in less than twenty-four hours—an app people loved. It was so unfair. She did everything right, and she still failed.

Allie punched the side of a locker bank with her fist. It didn't help at all. And now her hand was throbbing. She walked to her hiding spot by the student garden, tears still running down her cheeks, as she pulled out her phone and tapped on the Swap'd icon.

Everything was there. Thirty-two items to be bought, and sold, and fought over, in only two hours. One more auction, and she and Courtney would have all the money they needed. They'd buy the plane ticket that night. She'd tell Courtney what they'd been doing was illegal, and they'd shut Swap'd down for good. Ms. Slade would never have to know.

It would be so easy to get away with it.

But that's what she thought last time.

When things went wrong with Click'd, Allie had tried to fix it without telling anyone. She'd worked in the lab all through lunch and after school, and stayed up late every night, trying to find the glitch before anyone figured out what was going on. And it backfired in the worst possible way.

Allie stared at the queue. She knew what she had to do. And she hated it more than she could ever explain.

She highlighted the first item: ProperPrim's hair braiding with a starting bid of $5. She pressed the delete button and it disappeared.

She highlighted the second item: A video game Buh-Buy had posted with a starting bid of $40. She pressed the delete key.

She highlighted the next item: a rainbow-colored bath bomb posted by SparkleMotion.

And she kept going, highlighting items, feeling her stomach knot up every time she watched an item disappear. When she finally got to the DS, she let her finger hover over the delete key a moment longer than the others. But then she forced herself to press it.

Pretty soon, the queue was empty. Everything was gone. It was over as fast as it had begun.

No more Swap'd. No more chances to redeem herself in Naomi Ryan's eyes. No more plane ticket. No more Courtney.

thirty-one

Allie walked home from school. It was over three miles, and a lot of it was uphill, but she didn't care. It was a lot better than sitting on Bus #14, listening to everyone wonder why the clock hit 3:30 p.m. and the auction never began.

She tried to FaceTime Courtney to tell her what happened, but she couldn't bring herself to do it. She'd been so excited about meeting Marcus in the library, but now, she couldn't bear the idea of tutoring him, either. She sent him a text:

**Need to cancel our
session today. Sorry**

Now she was standing in her room, staring at Courtney's name on her phone, but as hard as she tried, she couldn't bring herself to start the FaceTime call. She tossed her phone on her bed and paced the floor again. Bo was on her heels, trying desperately to keep up, as she practiced what she was going to say for what seemed like the hundredth time.

"I should just tell her, right, Bo?"

He looked up at her.

"You're right. I just need to call and tell her what happened."

But it still took another full minute before she pressed the button.

Courtney answered right away. "There you are! I've been texting you!"

Allie had seen them all the way home. She'd been ignoring them. The last one read, *I made $28. How did you do?*

Allie couldn't bear to tell her she'd made nothing. That she'd killed the game. That they were still short.

Courtney didn't give her a chance to say anything. "Okay, so . . . I was just talking to my mom and filling her in on everything." The family photos that lined Courtney's hallway blurred by in the background. Allie watched her close her bedroom door and flop down on her bed. "My mom's going to buy it on her credit card and we'll give her the cash. Sound good?" She bounced in place. "I can't believe this is happening! It's all *actually* happening!"

Allie tried to speak, but she couldn't get the words past the knot in her throat.

"Oh, and my mom wants to talk to your mom about picking me up at the airport, and getting me back home, and all that other stuff. So, fill me in! How much did you get for the DS?"

Allie didn't know what to say. This wasn't at all the way she'd practiced it. She slid off her bed, onto the floor, and put her head in her hands. Bo settled in next to her and she buried her fingers in his fur. Here goes, she thought.

"We don't have the money."

The smile slipped from Courtney's face. "What?"

Allie didn't want to repeat it. It was hard enough to say it the first time.

"I had to cancel today's auction."

Courtney stared at her in disbelief. The look on her face made Allie feel one hundred times worse than she already did. "Why would you do that?"

Allie told Courtney all about her demo with Ms. Slade, and how it had been going so well until it went so wrong. "I didn't mention that I'd already taken it live. She would have freaked out if I told her I'd sold more than a thousand dollars' worth of stuff over the last three days!"

"Wait . . . She doesn't know?" Courtney asked. "Then why did you cancel it?"

"Because I had no other choice. It's not only against school rules, it's illegal in California! I couldn't hold another auction and risk getting caught."

"But we were this close!" Courtney held her thumb and forefinger together. "We could have made the money, bought my ticket, and then shut the whole game down before she ever found out." Courtney jumped off her bed. "There's still time. Hold it tonight! Send a message to everyone and tell them it's back on."

"I can't do that!"

"Sure, you can. Think about it. It's after hours. You're not selling anything on campus right now, are you?"

"No, but I'd have to do all the pickups at school tomorrow."

"Not if you change it. Have people come to your house after school with money and do the exchange there. Then you're not breaking any rules." Courtney was talking faster now. "Allie, look at me. We are forty-five dollars away from my plane ticket. That's it. Forty-five bucks! Think about all we've done this week! We can't stop now!"

"We have to stop now," Allie whispered.

Allie knew what it was like to have an out-of-control app. She remembered that look on Ms. Slade's face when she told her she knew Click'd had a glitch, and that she'd kept it going anyway. She'd never forget it. She wasn't about to keep Swap'd alive and risk seeing her favorite teacher look at her that way again. "Always make new mistakes," Ms. Slade liked to say. She'd forgive Allie for making that mistake once, but not twice.

Courtney bit down on her lip. And then she shook her head hard. "You might have to stop, but I don't. Different school, different rules . . ."

"Courtney—" Allie began, but she wasn't listening.

"Ms. Slade told you it was illegal in California. I don't live in California."

Allie couldn't believe what she was hearing. "You know if it's against the law here, it probably is there, too."

"Maybe it is, but no one's told me that yet. As far as I'm concerned, this conversation never happened." She waved her finger back and forth between the two of them.

Courtney was up now, walking around her room, opening closet doors and desk drawers, and peeking under her bed.

"What are you doing?"

"Looking for something I can sell for at least forty-five bucks." She stopped moving. And then she walked straight to her desk. "Got it." She held her brand-new game controller up in front of her. "I'm selling this."

"But you just got that for Christmas. You've been wanting that controller forever."

"I guess I want to see you even more." Courtney's voice hitched, and Allie could tell she was fighting back tears. "Too bad you don't feel the same about me."

"What?"

Courtney looked right at the phone. "You should have sold the DS. I never cared about your stupid bet to open all the racers. If you'd sold it last week, we would be at least thirty dollars richer. And we would have bought my ticket over the weekend, before the price went up, and none of this would be happening!"

"So this is all my fault?"

"Well it's not mine!" Courtney yelled. And then she narrowed her eyes and said, "R.O.B."

"What?"

"R.O.B. is the last unlockable character in Mario Kart. There. Now you know."

And then the screen went dark.

Five minutes later, Allie was still staring off into the distance, wondering what to do, when her mom knocked on her door and poked her head inside.

"Hey, what was all the shouting about in here?"

Allie couldn't speak. She couldn't move.

Her mom stepped into her room and sat on her bed. "What's going on?"

That was all it took. A tear slid down her cheek, followed by another one, and another one. She sat down next to her mom and buried her face in her shoulder.

Her mom pulled Allie in close. "Talk to me."

And Allie did. She told her everything. She even told her how she'd cheated on the tutoring sessions she sold to Marcus, and that made her start crying all over again. And then she took a deep breath, dried her eyes, and collected herself before she got to the worst part: the conversation she had with Ms. Slade that afternoon.

The two of them talked for a long time. They came up with a plan. And by the time they were finished, Allie was exhausted in every way. Her mom made her go downstairs for dinner, but thankfully, her parents didn't make her talk.

Later that night, her mom brought her tea and tucked her in.

"I'm so proud of you," her mom said. She kissed her forehead and pulled the covers up to her chin. "What you did took courage."

It didn't feel like courage.

"Don't think about it anymore. Give your body and brain a break, okay?"

Allie didn't fight her. She couldn't. She closed her eyes and let sleep take over.

She didn't realize until she woke up the next morning that she hadn't started good day/bad day, and Courtney hadn't either.

And just like that, their 170-day streak was broken.

tuesday

thirty-two

Allie's mom drove her to school so she wouldn't have to take the bus. She was afraid if she heard all the chatter about Swap'd, it would make it impossible for her to do what she knew she had to do.

They arrived early, and the campus was still quiet. Her mom pulled into the roundabout and stopped the car. "Are you okay?" she asked.

"Yeah," Allie said, but she wasn't totally sure it was true.

"You did the right thing."

Allie had lost count of how many times her mom had said it. And she wished it made her feel better, but it didn't. Then again, at that point, she couldn't think of anything that would. She got out of the car, waved good-bye, and walked to the lab.

Ms. Slade was already there, sitting at her desk, her fingers typing fast on the keyboard.

"Ms. Slade," Allie said.

Her teacher stopped typing and looked at her. "Good morning. You're here early."

"I have to tell you something." Her voice broke on the last word. "It's important."

Ms. Slade stood and met Allie halfway, and then led her over to the green velvet couch in the corner of the room. It was covered in throw pillows with funny sayings on them, like *Video games have prepared me for the zombie apocalypse* and *Come to the nerd side, we have π.*

Ms. Slade sat next to her. The red Lego blocks she was wearing as earrings swung back and forth.

"Do you remember my friend, Courtney, from CodeGirls Camp last summer?" Allie began. "She was my roommate, and she was on stage with me during my Click'd presentation."

"I remember," Ms. Slade said.

"I got to camp not knowing a single person, but Courtney and I clicked immediately. She was my best friend that summer, and she's still one of my best friends. We talk every day—four, even five times a day. We've been missing each other like crazy, and last week, when I told her I got two tickets for Game On Con, we came up with a plan to get her here, so she could come with me. She's a huge gamer."

"I see." Ms. Slade's eyebrows pinched together, like she was trying to figure out where Allie was going with all of this.

"We asked our parents to fly her out here, but the plane ticket was four hundred dollars, and they said no. They said the two of us should figure out a way to get her here on our own. And then you told us about the reuse assignment. Courtney and I built Swap'd so we could make money fast and buy Courtney a plane ticket to San Francisco."

Ms. Slade's expression changed, as if all the puzzle pieces in her mind were falling into place.

"We already rolled it out. Last week, here at Mercer and at her school. I held the first auction on Wednesday, the second on Thursday, and the third on Friday."

"You already held three auctions?"

Allie nodded. "I sold over a thousand dollars' worth of stuff. I would have sold another five hundred yesterday, but I canceled the auction."

"Why didn't you tell me all this earlier?" she asked.

Allie forced out an exhale. "I wanted to. But Courtney and I were so close. I couldn't imagine shutting it down, but . . . I did." Allie reached into her backpack for the list she and her mom had printed out the night before, sorted by real name, and complete with item, buyer, seller, amount, locker number, and avatar name. The list contained seventy-four items, sold for a total of $1,163, along with Allie's earnings.

"Well, that's impressive. Against the rules, but still impressive." Ms. Slade studied the list. She set it down on her lap and locked her eyes on Allie's. "I'm really proud of you."

Her mom had been saying that since she told her the night before, but it sounded different hearing it come from her teacher's mouth. Allie felt the tears well up in her eyes again.

"For what?" Allie asked.

She started listing them using her fingers. "First, because you absolutely aced this assignment. I can't believe you came up with something so complex, but solid and user-friendly, in such a short time. Second, because you came up with an ingenious way to get something you wanted. I like that. And third, because you shut it down *before* it became problematic." Ms. Slade rested her hand on Allie's shoulder. "You did the right thing."

Allie felt a huge lump in her throat. She swallowed hard, but it wouldn't go away.

"And now, we have to fix it."

"How?" Allie asked.

"Well, we basically need to go back in time. We've got to put everything back the way it was before." She waved the list in the air. "We're going to return everyone's cash and all the items to their respective sellers, and we're going to pretend this never happened. I'll have to tell Mr. Mohr, of course, but I think he'll be okay with that solution. How about you? Are you okay with that?"

Allie kind of expected Ms. Slade to say that, but she still wished she hadn't. She thought about Courtney and her Swap'd queue, full of stuff. If she sold even half of it, they'd have all they needed to buy her ticket. She wished Ms. Slade would yell at her but let her keep the money, rather than act so calm and make her give it all back.

"I can't keep it?"

Ms. Slade shook her head.

Allie held her breath as she reached into her backpack and took out the envelope containing all the cash she'd collected since that first wad of bills fell out of her locker and onto her shoe the Thursday before. She bit on her lip to keep from crying as she handed it to her teacher.

Ms. Slade turned it over in her hands a few times.

"Okay, here's what we're going to do." She stood and walked to her desk. She returned holding a little jar of paper clips and a stack of happy-looking yellow Post-its. "We're going to deal with the sellers first. Go sit in the back and figure out how much money we need to give back to each one. I have a class right now, but I'm free during second period. We'll call each person in, return the ten percent you took, and then tell them who bought their item and how much they need to return. Then we'll call in the buyers and figure out how we're going to get all the merchandise back to its original owner over the next few days."

"What if they don't have the money anymore?"

"We'll figure that out as we need to." She pointed at a desk in the back corner. "Get to work."

Allie stood. She walked to the back of the room in a daze, sat down at her desk, and started organizing everything. Before the bell rang, she pulled out her phone and launched Courtney's version of Swap'd. Everything was still there in the queue, loaded and ready to start at 3:30 p.m. sharp.

The bell rang, and the first period students filled the room. Allie hid in the corner creating stacks of cash, clipping them together, and marking the seller's name with a Post-it. She was so deep in thought, she didn't realize class was over until the bell rang again. And then it was time to return everything.

Ms. Slade pushed two desks together at the front of the room. "Have a seat here, Allie."

Allie did what she was told.

"I'll be calling each person from class and asking them to come here to the lab. I'll have them wait outside and send them in one at a time." She picked up her phone, dialed the office, and said, "Okay, we're ready."

Over the next forty-five minutes, each seller came into the lab and sat across from Allie. Ms. Slade explained things. Allie was quick with her explanation and her apologies. And then she slid an envelope filled with cash across the desk.

Maddie was visibly shaken. Zoe looked furious on Allie's behalf. Nathan just took his envelope and left, like he didn't know what to say. And when Emma came in, she hugged Allie hard and refused to take the cash. "Keep it," she whispered.

"I can't," Allie whispered back.

It was a nice thought, but it wasn't as if Emma's ten percent made a huge difference. Allie's take on all the slime Emma had sold came to $4.50.

And then the buyers came in. Allie knew many of them, and the rest she recognized from the locker pickups. Cassie said she'd return Nathan's headset, and Evan and Nick agreed to return all the games they bought. Cassidy already used one of the bath bombs, but she said she'd return the room spray. Kathryn planned to give back the candles. All the fidget spinners were heading back to their original owners.

It wasn't great, but it wasn't too horrible. Not until Marcus stepped into the lab.

Allie shifted in her chair, and she was pretty sure she was going to throw up as she heard Ms. Slade say, "Have a seat, Mr. Inouye."

Allie picked at her fingernails. She bit her lip. She crossed and re-crossed her legs. The clock seemed to slow to a crawl as she waited for Marcus to cross the room and take the seat facing her. Allie gripped the sides of her chair.

"Thanks for coming in," Ms. Slade began as she had

with all the others. "Let me explain what's going on." She filled him in quickly and then scanned the list. "It looks like you bought . . . tutoring sessions?"

"From me," Allie said. "Three anonymous Spanish tutoring sessions held online. To . . . help him pass a big test."

Ms. Slade looked at Marcus and then back at Allie. "How many tutoring sessions did you hold?"

"Two," Marcus said.

She consulted the paper in front of her. "So, how did you do on the test?" Ms. Slade asked.

"I got an A."

Allie beamed. "You did?"

Marcus nodded, but he didn't smile back. "Yeah."

Ms. Slade was all business. "Well, this one is easy. Allie, you owe Marcus a twenty-eight-dollar refund."

Allie reached over for the paper-clipped bundle of bills and slid it to Marcus. He didn't pick it up. He didn't even look at her.

"So," Marcus finally said. "Everyone knows." He kept his gaze on the desk. "All your friends. They know it was me."

Allie nodded. She felt sick all over again. "Yeah. I mean, Zoe knows. And Maddie and Emma. And . . . Chris."

"Zoe knows?" he asked.

Allie nodded again. "She helped me write the post."

Marcus's expression changed. He no longer looked mad. Now he looked embarrassed. And maybe even a little . . . hurt. He grabbed the cash, stood, and jammed it into his pocket. "So much for being anonymous." Before Allie could say anything else, he stood and walked to the door. He didn't turn around.

Ms. Slade put a checkmark next to his name. Allie felt small. She couldn't imagine this getting any worse. Until she heard Ms. Slade say, "Have a seat, Ms. Gilbert."

Kelsey Gilbert slipped into the seat across from her, and Allie froze. Suddenly, she was face-to-face with the other mistake she'd made. The one she'd tried to forget all about.

Allie listened to Ms. Slade list off the things Kelsey had purchased over the last three days. A necklace. An iPhone case. A bag of candy. She explained that she needed to return them to the owner.

Allie watched her, wondering if Kelsey realized that *she* was Princess Peach. She was the game's creator. The only one with access to the system. And also the one who sold the tutoring sessions and made sure Kelsey didn't win them.

She wanted to tell her, and she knew she *should* tell her, but Allie couldn't bring herself to say the words. When Ms. Slade finally excused her, Allie started breathing normally again.

"Let's take a little break. I'm going to get a coffee. How about some popcorn?" Ms. Slade asked. When Allie shook her head, Ms. Slade scooted her chair closer. "You know, I've found that warm, buttery popcorn is a good start to fixing just about anything."

Allie ran her fingernail through a deep groove in the desk and didn't look up. "Not this."

"Yes, even this," Ms. Slade said, resting her hand on Allie's shoulder. "Look, I know you feel horrible. This whole thing seems enormous right now. But I promise you, it won't feel like this forever. People will forget all about it. They'll move on. And you . . . well, you'll take what you need from this whole experience, and you'll move on, too. It's okay."

Allie took the deepest breath, like she was inhaling all the words Ms. Slade had just said and storing them deep in her soul. It was exactly what she needed to hear. Especially those last ones. She could handle everyone else's reaction, as long as she knew her favorite teacher believed it was all going to be okay.

Allie nodded at Ms. Slade, already feeling better. "Thanks. And I'll take some popcorn, too."

thirty-three

Allie managed to avoid everyone for the rest of the day. She stayed in the lab during lunch, meeting with buyers and sellers, returning cash, and figuring out how to return the things they'd purchased. During advanced CS class, Ms. Slade made her take a break and go to the library. That was fine with Allie. That way, she didn't have to see Nathan.

At the end of the day, she walked toward the bus, but she stopped at the flagpole. She couldn't seem to take the steps to the door. She was relieved when Zoe stepped off the bus a few minutes later and walked toward her.

"Do you want me to walk home with you?"

Allie glanced up at the sky and then shook her head. "It's about to start raining again."

Zoe raised an eyebrow. "So then . . . maybe we should get on the bus." She didn't wait for Allie to answer, she just threaded her arm through hers and started leading her in that direction.

At the top of the steps, Allie glanced at Marcus. He kept his gaze fixed on something outside the window and didn't look at her.

When she got to her seat, Allie flopped down in her spot next to Zoe and pulled out her phone.

"What are you doing?" Zoe asked.

"Courtney's auction is over by now. Arizona is an hour ahead of us."

"She doesn't know you had to give all the money back?"

Allie shook her head.

On screen, Courtney's version of Swap'd launched. Allie expected to see a list of all the items that had sold and her updated leaderboard, but instead, there was a message on the screen:

TODAY'S AUCTION HAS BEEN CANCELED.

"Call her," Zoe said. "Now."

After the way the two of them left things the day before, Allie wasn't sure Courtney would even take her call, but she FaceTimed her anyway. She ducked down low, behind the

244

seat in front of her, shielding herself from the noise of the bus. It rang three times before Courtney finally picked up.

"Hi," Courtney said.

The background was unfamiliar. Courtney wasn't in her computer lab at school, and she wasn't in her bedroom. But Allie didn't say anything about it.

"Hi," she replied.

Zoe gave Allie's arm a supportive squeeze.

"You didn't do it," Allie finally said.

"I tried. At five minutes before the start time, I just . . . couldn't."

Allie had so much to tell her, but she didn't know where to start. The day still felt like a series of blurred memories—like it had all happened to someone else, not to her.

"I'm sorry I got so mad yesterday," Courtney finally said.

"It's okay," Allie said. "I'm sorry I didn't sell the DS last week. You were right. If I'd sold it, none of this would have happened."

Although she still would have had to tell Ms. Slade. She still would have had to return all the money.

"Look, it's all going to be okay. We're going to buy that plane ticket tonight after all. You'll never guess where I am right now!"

"Where?"

"My next-door neighbor asked if I wanted to baby-sit." Courtney turned the phone toward a little girl with a tiara on her head, sitting at a small table, surrounded by stuffed animals. "This is Parker. She's five and she's the cutest thing! We're having a tea party. I've been calling her Princess Peach, in your honor."

Zoe leaned in closer and said, "Hi, Parker." They both waved at the screen.

"Her mom's paying me forty bucks! It's a legit job. In two hours, I'll have the rest of the money to buy my ticket and get to Game On!" Courtney gave the phone screen a fist bump. "You were right. It all worked out."

Courtney was still waiting for Allie to tap her fist to the screen.

"What's wrong?" Courtney asked. "Did the price go up again? I didn't think to check!"

"That's not it." Allie hung her head, wishing she didn't have to say the words that were just sitting there, waiting to leave her mouth. "I had to give it all back. Everything. The stuff is gone. The cash is gone."

Courtney's face fell. "I should have held my auction today."

"We'd still be short."

"We'd still have *something*!"

"It wouldn't have mattered. You did the right thing, Courtney."

"Yeah? Well, it doesn't feel like the right thing. None of this feels right! We worked *so* hard."

Allie knew what she meant. Every time she had that thought, her chest felt uncomfortably tight.

Courtney sat there for the longest time, not saying anything. It was excruciating. Allie hated hearing her so upset, but the silence was even worse.

The little girl in the background held her cup in the air. "Our tea is getting cold."

"I'd better go," Courtney said.

"Okay." Allie hated everything about this. She didn't want Courtney to be mad at her anymore. She didn't want *anyone* to be mad at her anymore. "But we'll talk tonight, right? We'll do good day/bad day?"

"Yeah."

She hung up. She and Zoe were silent until the bus pulled to her stop. "See you," she whispered.

Marcus didn't look at her as she left the bus, and as she walked the half block to her house, she tried not to think about that. She tried not to think about what happened with Courtney, or what happened with Ms. Slade, or what happened with Kelsey.

She rounded the corner, stepped onto her lawn, and looked up to find a dog running straight for her. It took her a second to recognize him, but as soon as she did, she dropped her backpack on the grass, crouched down low, and threw out her arms.

"Archie!" He came at her so fast, he knocked her backward.

She sat up, laughing as he covered her cheeks with dog kisses.

"Sorry," Nathan said, trying to pull him away from her,

but Allie nuzzled in closer. After the day she'd had, this was, without question, the high point.

"It's okay." She scratched Archie's back and peered up at Nathan. "What are you doing here?"

"Can I talk to you?"

She was still mad at him for what he'd said in the lab the day before, but when she saw the look on his face, that anger started melting away. She'd never wanted to fight with him in the first place.

Nathan reached out his hand. Allie took it and let him pull to her feet.

"Always," she said.

thirty-four

Allie grabbed her backpack, and the two of them walked toward the house with Archie leading the way. As she searched for her keys, Bo barked and scratched at the other side of the door. As soon as she got it open, Bo and Archie raced straight for each other and started wrestling in the entryway. Allie and Nathan stepped over them on their way to the kitchen.

Allie poured two glasses of milk and grabbed a half-empty package of Oreos from the cabinet. She hopped up on the counter and Nathan joined her.

"What are you doing here?" Allie asked as she dunked her cookie into the milk and took a bite.

"Well, I didn't realize this until just now, but clearly, I'm here to show you the proper way to eat an Oreo." Nathan twisted his cookie apart, dunked one half into the milk, took a bite, and then dunked it again, finishing it off.

Allie rolled her eyes. "Dude. Everyone knows you only separate the cookie side from the frosted side when you have no milk. When you *do* have milk, you have to dunk the whole thing in and eat it together, because then you get the whole cookie-frosting-milk combo." She demonstrated her technique, and then took a bite, closed her eyes, and smiled as she chewed.

"That ruins the frosting. You, Allie Navarro, are a frosting *ruiner.*"

"A what?"

"You heard me."

He grabbed another cookie, twisted it apart, and licked the frosting.

"You are so weird."

"I know. So are you."

"True." Allie grabbed another Oreo, dunked it her way, and took a bite. "Why are you really here?"

"Well . . ." Nathan wiped his mouth with the back of his hand. "You know how you keep asking me what I'm building for the reuse project?"

"And you keep saying it's a surprise."

"Yeah. Well, I'm not building anything."

Allie stopped mid-dunk, looking up at him.

"Surprise!" He threw his arms in the air and pasted on a big grin.

Allie still hadn't moved. "What do you mean you're not building anything?"

"I mean, I'm not building anything. Because I can't. I haven't made anything new since I finished Built."

Allie thought back to all the months that had passed since Games for Good. He finished Built in September. It was almost the end of January. "We've had at least three development projects since then. What have you been working on?"

He shrugged. "Nothing. I keep making up some Built-related emergency I have to deal with. I've actually taken pieces of my own game apart and put them back together again so I wouldn't be lying to Slade when she asked what I was working on. She gave me full credit, since technically, I was coding, but now I think she's onto me. She told me I wasn't getting out of this assignment, no matter what. That if I didn't turn something new in, she'd be forced to give me an F."

"So what have you been doing for the last two weeks?"

"Hanging out with my friends. Doing homework. Binge-watching Netflix. Playing Fortnite. Finding stuff to sell on Swap'd. You know, the usual."

The pieces were all clicking into place. Allie couldn't believe she hadn't noticed sooner. All week, he'd been on the blacktop with his friends during lunch. She hadn't had to force him out of the computer lab once. He was even *late* to CS class a few times. She remembered thinking he looked so confident, so cocky, that he must have been way ahead of her, and building something extraordinary. As it turned out, it was the exact opposite.

"Is that why you've been playing basketball at lunch all week? Because you've been avoiding coding?"

"Pretty much."

"Why didn't you tell me?"

"I tried to. Last Thursday in the lab . . ." he trailed off. Allie thought back to that day. She remembered he'd started to ask her something, but then Zoe texted her, and she got all caught up in her tutoring auction item. He told her to forget about it. She had.

"I don't know what happened," Nathan continued. "For a couple of months after Games for Good, I was on top of the world. My Built user base was skyrocketing. My game was trending. Reporters were calling me every day, my picture was in the paper, and I got to go to all these meetings at Spyglass with real-life game developers. All of them were so excited about what I'd done. And then there were the sponsors, sending me free stuff all the time, practically begging me for a billboard in the game. It felt like it was the beginning of something big. And then"—he snapped his fingers—"like that, it was over. The users started dropping off, and the meeting invitations stopped coming, and the packages stopped magically arriving. It wasn't the beginning at all. It was just temporary. And now it's over."

At least he'd had his moment. She would have liked to have known what that was like, even if it was temporary.

"All I could think about was that I had to do something great. Something new and better, something that would get people's attention again. I can't even begin to tell you how many hours I spent in my room, late into the night, just staring in my monitor, with my fingers on the keyboard, unable to code a single line. And the more days that went by like that, the more I started to panic, and the more my mind started messing with me. What if I never come up with anything else?" Nathan slid off the counter and started pacing the kitchen floor. "What if I just had one decent idea, Allie, and that was it?"

"That's not going to happen. Something will come to you."

"What if it doesn't?"

"It will."

"How do you know?"

"Because I know *you!*" Allie couldn't hold back any longer. She slid off the counter and stood right in front of him. "Look, I've spent my whole life trying to beat you, and you're always a step ahead of me. You always have the better idea for the better user base or the better implementation—"

"That's not true," he said, cutting her off. "*You're* always the one I'm trying to beat."

"And you always do! I *always* come in second to you. I have since third grade."

Nathan's face fell. "You know I hate that, right? It's not fair. You always have better ideas. That dog-walking app?"

"Came in second to your weather app."

"And that puzzle game—"

"Came in second to *your* hoverboard game. And my soccer skills game came in second to your Quidditch-skills game."

"Okay, but Click'd—"

"Came in tenth!" Allie's voice cracked. "I failed so badly, I wasn't even allowed to be onstage with you!"

He looked right into her eyes. "You should have been up there. If you had been, you would have won. And *you* would have handled this whole thing so much better than I have. You wouldn't have coder's block because you were famous for, like, ten minutes and then you weren't."

"I might have!" Allie said.

"Well, here's your chance. Go to Game On, do that meet-and-greet with Naomi Ryan, show her Swap'd, and land a spot in the hackathon program. You deserve it. And you won't have to worry about me competing against you. I'm not even applying."

"That doesn't have anything to do with me, does it?" She brought her hands to her hips. "Because if there's any part of you, even a *tiny* part of you, that's staying out of this because you think that will help me get in . . ."

Nathan reeled back. "Of course not! This has nothing to do with you, Allie." Nathan combed his fingers through his hair. "I have nothing to show Naomi Ryan. I have nothing to show Ms. Slade on Friday. I have *nothing*! No app. No game. No users. Nothing to present. And now it's too late."

"No, it's not. You have, like, thirty hours. Courtney and I built Swap'd in about thirteen. You just need an idea."

"Ooh, got it!" He reached in his pocket and pretended to pull something out, but when he opened his hand, it was empty. "Oh, wait. Never mind."

Allie rolled her eyes. "What's your biggest problem with Built? Why are you losing users?"

"I don't know . . . I think it's just too complicated. It takes a while to learn. It scares new people away."

Allie paced the kitchen floor, walking back and forth between the sink and the fridge. He was right. It was complex in some ways, but it was also so cute, with its tiny houses, and the little builders in their overalls, and that store that sold all the building supplies. Those miniature billboards with the sponsorship signs were brilliant.

"Maybe you need something simpler, you know? A way to introduce people to the game in a friendly way."

"Like what?"

Allie paced some more. She paced and thought and paced and thought. She wondered how that town could scare anyone away. It was adorable, with its tree-lined sidewalks, and the town square, and all those cute little roads.

Roads.

Allie stopped and turned to Nathan. "I've got it. Follow me."

She took off, heading for the stairs. She took them two

at a time, with Nathan and Bo and Archie trailing after her, all trying to keep up. When she got to her room she flung the door open, went straight to her desk, and opened the top drawer.

She unzipped the white case, removed the DS, opened it up, and flicked the power button. As she handed it to Nathan, the Mario Kart theme song filled the room.

He smiled. "I haven't heard that song in years." And then he looked at the screen. "This is why your name is Princess Peach."

"Courtney was giving me a hard time for not knowing about the four bonus racers, so I've been playing it all week, trying to unlock them."

"Did you?"

"No." Allie tapped her fingernail on the screen. "But this is it. Make this for the assignment. You already have a map, you created it when you made Built. Start with that as your foundation and create a super-simple, two-person racing game through the streets of your virtual neighborhood."

Nathan stared at the screen. "It'll get people familiar with the game."

"Yep. And you'll be racing past billboards. You can sell those to completely new sponsors."

"At the end of the race, they'll have an invitation to join Built."

"Exactly. It's viral. Friends tell friends. It's a way to get new users, and get sponsors, Spyglass, and everyone else talking about it again."

Nathan looked at her. "See, I told you. You have better ideas."

Allie shot him a grateful smile and then took her seat at her computer. She opened a new workspace. "I've got a lot more than that."

She picked up her phone, opened the CodeGirls group text, and fired off a message. Less than ten minutes later, her workspace started filling up with code. All Nathan had to do was take his map, snap it together with the new stuff from the CodeGirls, and connect it all together to create something completely new.

Nathan's jaw fell as he stared at the screen. "What just happened?" he asked.

Allie looked over her shoulder at him. "You asked for help."

wednesday

thirty-five

Allie let out a yawn as the bus squealed to a stop in front of her. She climbed the steps and turned at the landing, trying not to make eye contact with Marcus.

"Hey, Three," he said.

She paused. "Hey, Six."

"Can I talk to you when we get to school?"

Her heart started beating harder. She wanted to answer him, but she couldn't think straight with it thwacking against her ribs like that.

"Yeah, sure," she said, trying to sound nonchalant about the whole thing. "Meet at the flagpole?"

Marcus nodded.

"Take your seat, Ms. Navarro," Mr. Steve yelled.

Allie walked to her seat on wobbly legs. As soon as she sat down, the bus lurched forward.

"Wait, what just happened?" Zoe whispered.

"He wants to talk to me about something."

"What?"

"How would I know?" Allie glanced up at Marcus. He was staring out the window.

Zoe bounced in her seat. "That's good!"

"How do you know it's *good*?"

"Well, I don't, I guess. But look on the bright side!" Zoe said.

"There's a bright side?"

"You just officially said more than three words to him. In person! And now you're about to have a real conversation. It's perfect. And you have me to thank!" Zoe smacked Allie's arm with the back of her hand. "Why don't you look happy?"

None of it felt right. It felt weird, and awkward, and scary, and it certainly didn't feel perfect. Her heart was thumping against her rib cage, and her palms were sweaty, just like they'd been when she and Marcus were sitting with Ms. Slade in the lab the day before.

Allie wished she could have gone back in time and never sold that tutoring item. That would have been easier than facing him.

Ten minutes later, the bus pulled into the roundabout

and stopped. Everyone rushed for the doors. Allie tried to stand, but her legs were still shaky. She gripped the seat in front of her and waited for everyone to pass by.

"Aw, look how cute he is, waiting for you and playing with that little string on his hoodie," Zoe said. Allie followed her gaze. Marcus was sitting on the small brick wall surrounding the flagpole. "I might be changing my mind about the dimples. That boy *is* pretty adorable."

"Not helping."

Mr. Steve cleared his throat from the driver's seat. "Time to go, ladies."

"Come on," Zoe said, nudging Allie with her shoulder. "I can't move until you do."

Mr. Steve stood and turned to face them. "You know, I get paid to pick you up, drive you to school, and let you out. That's how it works. That's why they pay me the big bucks. I lose my job if I return to the bus yard with children still on board."

"Sass," Zoe said as she grabbed Allie's arm and forced her to stand. "That's why I've always liked you, Mr. Steve." She gave Allie a light shove, urging her toward the door. "Go. Chicken."

"What if he's still mad at me for telling you guys about the tutoring thing?"

"Then you'll apologize."

"Okay, but what if he's *still* mad?"

"He'll get over it, Allie. He's really nice, I swear. It'll

be fine. Go tell him why you did it—because you *like* him. He'll understand. How can he be mad if you tell him the truth?"

"I can't tell him that," she whispered.

Zoe probably thought Allie was too shy to admit it, but that wasn't it. She couldn't tell Marcus she liked him, because deep down, she was no longer sure it was true.

The flirting was fun. She loved that her friends were so invested in her mission. The buildup was exciting, and the thought of seeing him every day made her giddy. But until Maddie made that comment outside the store a few days earlier, Allie had never really thought about what happened next. She wasn't sure how she felt about the two of them as a couple. And, as nice as he was, she was starting to think that she liked the *idea* of Marcus more than she actually liked *him*.

Zoe shook her head dismissively. "That's just the nerves talking."

Allie reluctantly made her feet move, and somehow, she made it down the steps and onto the sidewalk. As the bus pulled away, Zoe hugged her and said, "I'll be waiting right over there. Tell me *everything*."

She took off, leaving Allie alone. Marcus was watching her. She had no choice but to walk toward him.

She sat on the wall, keeping a bit of distance between them. "Hey, Six."

"Hey, Three," he said.

He kept playing with that string on his hoodie.

Allie fidgeted with her fingernails.

"I have something for you," he said.

"You do?"

He reached into his backpack and pulled out the gift bag filled with all the items Allie had gathered up with the help of Nathan and her friends. "These are yours."

Allie wondered if that was the only reason he wanted to talk to her. She tried not to look disappointed as she took the bag. "Thanks."

The two of them were quiet again.

Allie knew it was her turn to talk. She took a deep breath, gathering her nerve, and then said, "I'm sorry, Marcus. Really. Technically, I didn't tell my friends who you were. They knew before I uploaded the auction. We were all hoping you'd buy it, and when you did . . ." Allie trailed off. She wasn't sure what to say next. She'd already given too much away. She pulled her thoughts together and kept going. "You have every right to be mad at me."

"I'm not. I mean, I was. But I'm not anymore." He wrapped the string from his hoodie around his finger again. "Actually, I was never really *mad*, I was more . . . embarrassed, I guess."

Allie nodded. She understood that feeling.

"Did Zoe put you up to it?" he asked.

Allie looked at him out of the corner of her eye. "Actually, she did. How did you know that?"

"She's in my Spanish class. We're in the same group and she kept telling me I should bid on the tutoring sessions, so . . . actually, I thought she was Princess Peach. I bought the auction item because I've been trying to ask her out for months, and I thought maybe the tutoring would give me a chance to talk to her . . ."

Allie's heart sank deep in her chest. "What?"

He hid behind his hand. "I know. Lame, right?"

Allie shrugged. "It's not *that* lame."

"Anyway." He lowered his hand and looked at her again. "I thought Zoe was trying to get me to buy them, and then we'd have this inside joke. But then when I found out it was you, I felt like *I* was the joke. Like you, and Zoe, and all your friends had been laughing at me behind my back the whole time."

"We weren't," Allie said. "I promise. We'd never do that."

Part of her was sad that he liked her friend and not her, but then she reminded herself about what she'd just admitted: Allie wasn't sure she *liked* him—liked him anyway.

"I know. It took me a while to get over it, but I realized that wasn't the case at all. You were just offering tutoring sessions because you're actually a really good tutor."

Allie sat a little taller. "I am?"

"The best. You made that so much fun. And I told you, I got an A on my test. I haven't gotten an A on anything in that class all year!"

Allie's heart didn't feel quite so broken anymore. She still hated being rejected, but knowing he thought she was a good tutor made her feel a little better about the whole thing.

"Over the weekend, I told my mom about our sessions and bag full of stuff," Marcus continued. "And then last night, when my mom saw that A, I thought she was going to jump straight out of her skin. She was so happy."

The look of pride on his face was impossible to miss. And it must have been as contagious as Courtney's laugh, because suddenly, Allie felt it radiating all through her body.

"She wants you to keep tutoring me."

That jolted her back. "Excuse me?"

"She said she'll pay fifteen dollars a session. She suggested we meet twice a week, maybe in the library. Or you could ride the bus to my house and she'd take you home afterward. She gave me money to give to you, but I figured I'd better not hand it to you on school grounds." He reached down and patted his backpack.

"That's probably smart." Allie let out a nervous laugh that didn't even sound like her own.

"What do you think?"

"I think that sounds amazing."

She had a job. A job that would pay thirty dollars a week. In a few months, she'd have enough money to help Courtney buy a ticket.

"Do you mind if we start next week?" she asked. "This week has been kind of bananas."

"You mean *plátanos.*"

"Yes, exactly. *Plátanos.*" She gave him a fist bump. "Nice."

The bell rang. Marcus stood up quickly. Allie thought

he was going to leave, but he lingered for a long moment, shifting his weight. "Hey, I also wanted to tell you that I'm really sorry about what happened to you yesterday. I can't believe you had to give all that money back. That must have sucked."

"Pretty much," Allie said. "But it's okay. I'm glad you're not mad at me. And I'm sorry about telling my friends who you were. I won't tell anyone I'm tutoring you this time, I promise."

He rocked back on his heels. "It's okay. I don't care if people know anymore. But will you do me a favor and keep the Zoe thing to yourself?"

"Deal." Allie slid her finger and thumb across her lips, like she was zipping them closed.

He smiled. "See ya, Allie."

"See ya, Marcus."

As soon as he was gone, Zoe ran across the lawn. "What happened?" she asked.

"He wants me to keep tutoring him," she said.

"See, I told you!" She threaded her arm through Allie's and started leading her toward first period. "This is the part where you thank me."

"Thank you," Allie said. "But I think Marcus and I are just going to be friends."

Zoe stopped cold. "What? Why?"

"I don't know." Allie shrugged. "It just doesn't feel right."

"After all that?"

"Yep," Allie said. "I mean, he doesn't like dogs. How can I like someone who doesn't like *dogs*?" And then she bumped her hip against Zoe's. "Something tells me it will all turn out for the best."

As they walked to class, Allie thought about everything that had just happened with Marcus. And suddenly, a new idea started forming in her mind. It didn't fix the mess she'd made, and it didn't get Courtney a plane ticket in time for Game On, but it was a good start.

By the time she slid into her seat in math class, she knew exactly what she needed to do.

thirty-six

At lunch, Allie ran straight to the lab. She had been so focused on Swap'd, she hadn't even thought to open Click'd, but she logged in and navigated over to the backend database like it was second nature. Within minutes, she was staring at the list of every Click'd user—934 names, and nearly every student at Mercer Middle School.

She scrolled down to the G's and stopped at Gilbert.

Kelsey's photo was in the upper left-hand corner, next to her name and bio. Allie could see all her answers to the quiz questions, and her leaderboard featuring her top ten clicks.

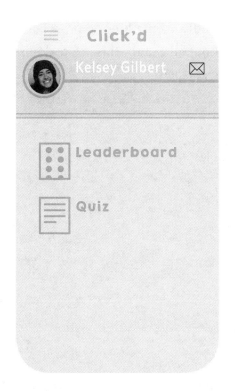

She tapped on the TEXT icon, and typed her message:

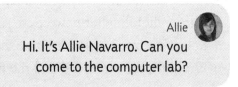

Allie
Hi. It's Allie Navarro. Can you
come to the computer lab?

Allie pressed SEND. While she waited, she opened a new file and started the second part of her new project. She found the perfect image, wrote a catchy headline and a clear description, and then she played with the fonts. She wanted something friendly. Something approachable. Something that said "fun" but also said, "this is a real business."

Her phone chirped.

Kelsey

Am I in trouble?

Allie

No! Not at all!

OK give me 5

Allie quickly picked a font, read the whole flyer one more time, and pressed PRINT. By the time the lab door opened and Kelsey stepped inside, Allie was standing at the printer, holding her newest creation.

Kelsey's gaze traveled around the room, taking in the workstations, the monitors, and the posters on the walls. "I didn't even know this room existed until yesterday. I walk right past it on the way to science every day."

"It's been here for years." Allie started walking toward the back of the room and motioned for Kelsey to follow her. "I want to show you something." She pulled out the chair in front of one of the two massive computers at the back of the

room—the ones Ms. Slade reserved for special projects—
and told Kelsey to have a seat as she powered it up.

Allie hadn't been back at that station since the fiasco
with Click'd, and as she sat down, she suddenly missed
those days when it was just Nathan and her, plowing
through lines of code and bags of microwave popcorn,
while they each listened to music on their headphones and
tried to ignore the other's presence. It was hard to believe
it had only been four months earlier. It was even harder to
believe that back then, they hated each other.

"This is Ira," Allie said, patting the top of the monitor.
"In the old Wonder Woman TV show, Ira is the name of
the computer she uses to create false records for her secret
identity, Diana Prince."

Kelsey smiled as she ran her hand along the keyboard.
"I'm kind of obsessed with Wonder Woman. I've seen that
movie at least twenty times."

"I figured," Allie said. "I thought it was a brilliant avatar
name. It made it even harder for me to do what I did."

Kelsey looked confused. "What did you do?"

"I auctioned off those Spanish tutoring sessions you
almost won. Erm, well . . . *might* have won. *Should* have won,
but—"

Kelsey interrupted her. "You stopped it early." She sat
up a little straighter. "There was still time on the clock."

"Three seconds." Allie felt that same twist in her stomach. "You were bidding against this guy and—"

"You wanted him to win," Kelsey said, finishing Allie's

sentence. "So you ended it before I could raise the bid?"

Allie nodded.

Kelsey stared at her, and Allie couldn't read her expression. And then the corners of her mouth turned up in a small smile. "Diana Prince never would have done that, you know?"

Allie let out an uncomfortable laugh. "No, she wouldn't."

"Especially not for a guy."

"Never for a guy."

Allie grabbed a flyer from the stack and handed it to Kelsey. "I blew it, but I want to make it right."

Take your Español grade from **malo** to **excelente**!

Spanish tutoring by Allie

"You're tutoring?"

Allie shrugged. "In my spare time. When I'm not writing apps that get me into trouble."

"You seem to have a knack for that."

"I know, right?" Allie tapped the flyer with her fingertip. "I owe you. The first three sessions are on me."

Kelsey read the description. "Actually, I could really use it. We had a verbal exam yesterday and I totally bombed it. My mom always said I had an ear for languages. She's so wrong."

"That's not true. I'll prove it to you." Allie handed her more flyers. "Here. Give these to your friends in Spanish class. I'll prove it to all of you."

"Thanks. I will." Kelsey slipped them into her backpack. "So . . . did it work?" she asked.

"What?"

"You and the guy?"

Allie pictured Marcus holding up each item and snapping a picture. The apple. The balloon. The dollhouse chair. The flashlight. It felt like flirting at the time, and it was. Only Marcus thought he was flirting with Zoe.

"Not exactly," Allie said. "But it's okay."

"Tell me who he is, and maybe I can help." Kelsey winked at her. "I should probably check your references anyway . . . make sure you're a good tutor."

Allie brought her thumb and forefinger to her lips and turned an imaginary key, like she was locking them shut. "His secret identity is safe with me."

Kelsey shot her an approving smile as she turned to leave. "Now you're talking like someone who deserves to use Diana's computer."

thirty-seven

"I'm coming to San Francisco," Courtney said the second Allie answered the phone.

"For Game On?"

"I wish. Not that soon. But I'll be there." Courtney was bouncing in place. "Parker loved me! Her mom asked me to babysit twice a week after school. If I save every penny, I should be able to come for spring break."

"Or even sooner!" Allie yelled. "I got a job, too. Tutoring Spanish. Right now, I only have two students, Marcus and Kelsey, and well, technically, I'm not making any money on Kelsey right away, but still, I'll have money."

They propped their phones next to their keyboards,

and each opened a browser to one of the online ticketing services. Allie typed in the dates and entered the data into the empty fields:

From: Phoenix

To: San Francisco

Departure date: March 15

She hit the ENTER button, and then waited while the icon spun in place and the system searched for the lowest fare. Times, flight numbers, and prices appeared, and soon, they heard the celebratory sound as the "fabulous fare" landed at the top of the screen.

Allie angled her phone so Courtney could see what she was seeing.

"Two *hundred* dollars? That's it?"

"That's it," Allie said.

The two of them silently stared at the number, taking it in.

But it wasn't why Allie had called. She'd let go of her first secret at school that day. Now it was time to come clean on the second one.

Allie shifted nervously in her chair. "I have something to tell you," she blurted out.

"What's that?" Courtney asked, still staring at her own monitor.

"Have you heard about Spyglass Games' new teen hackathon program?"

"No, but I love hackathons. My dad and I did one about a year ago. It was a blast."

"They're creating a series of summer hackathons exclusively for teens, and they need participants to help build and shape the program. I've been trying to decide if I'm going to apply...."

"Why wouldn't you?"

"Because it's a *summer* program. I can't do that *and* go to CodeGirls Camp."

Courtney's face fell. "Oh."

"And ... there's something else."

Courtney didn't look too eager to hear it.

"The Game On passes include a meet-and-greet with Naomi Ryan."

Courtney's eyes grew wider. "Naomi Ryan? The CEO of Spyglass Games? How could you not tell me that part?"

Allie sucked in a breath. "I always planned to ... I just wasn't sure how to tell you about the meet-and-greet without also telling you I was applying to Hackathon. They want me to demo my latest game..." She trailed off.

"And you want to demo Swap'd?"

Hearing Courtney say it made Allie feel a hundred times worse. "Yeah ... ironic, right? If the selection committee loves the game you and I built together, and I got into Hackathon, it would keep me away from you this summer. But don't worry, it's super competitive. The chances of me getting in are, like, next to nothing."

"But if you *did* get in ... you'd go?"

Allie hesitated. It wasn't that she didn't want to tell Courtney. She was hesitating because she honestly didn't know the answer. She thought about how fun it would be to spend the summer at the Spyglass campus—eating lunches in the fancy cafeteria, attending brainstorming sessions with the developers, creating something totally new. And then she thought about the Fuller University campus—spending late nights in the Fishbowl and taking breaks to kick around a soccer ball with Courtney, and Kaiya, and Shonna, and Rachel, and all the others. She couldn't imagine her summer without them.

"Allie." Courtney waved her hand in front of the screen, interrupting her thoughts.

"Yeah."

"If you got in, you'd go! You'd *have* to go. You can't pass up a chance to spend the summer at Spyglass. I won't *let* you!"

"You wouldn't be mad?"

Courtney didn't even hesitate. "Mad? Of course not. We'd still talk all the time. We'd still do good day/bad day every night. And Fuller University isn't that far away from San Francisco. You could come visit us on the weekends. I'd miss you like crazy, but this is a chance of a lifetime, Allie. If you don't get in, that's one thing, but you have to try!"

"Really?" Allie could barely believe what Courtney was saying. But as it all hit her, she began to feel different . . . lighter.

"Of course!"

Allie had been wondering if she should apply for months, but now, she couldn't wait to open the application and press that SEND button. There was no longer a doubt in her mind. Except for one thing.

"I don't have anything new to demo."

"Sure you do; you have Swap'd. They'll love it. It's an awesome game with an even better backstory. Built in less than twenty-four hours using existing code from five kick-butt girls. Allie, you're in, no question!"

"I can't show them our *failed* game!"

"Failed game?" Courtney said. "Hey, Swap'd may have failed to get me to San Francisco, but it did *not* fail. We can't play it on a school campus, but it's an awesome app. Timed auctions? A leaderboard? People will love it! We just need to switch a few things up."

Allie started to see where Courtney was going with this. She began to picture it in her mind. "We'd need a payment engine," she said.

"And users will have to deal with shipping on their own," Courtney added.

"But we could snap all that in," Allie said. "I bet Spyglass could even help us get partners."

"Exactly," Courtney said. "Naomi Ryan doesn't need to know about the things that went wrong. She only needs to know what went right."

Courtney had a point. The two of them had killed the assignment. They hadn't just created a *working* game, they'd created a game people loved, one that kept them coming back, and one that was profitable. And they'd built it in less than twenty-four hours, working collaboratively, using chunks of code from girls who live all across the country.

Allie pictured Ms. Slade and her bucket of Legos. It was just the kind of thing Naomi Ryan would love.

"You're right. We have an amazing game and an even more amazing story." Allie took a big swig from her water bottle, and that's when the idea hit her. She wasn't sure why she hadn't thought of it earlier. "Courtney, you should apply, too! Maybe we'll both get in."

Courtney looked at her sideways. "Where would I stay?"

"You can spend the summer here at our house, with my family and me. We'll take the train to the campus every day together. It'll be just like camp, but even better!"

Allie could tell Courtney was thinking seriously about it. "I *might* apply, but right now, we have more important things to focus on."

"We do?"

"Yep. We need to build your demo for Saturday. You're going to have to present Swap'd for both of us."

thursday

thirty-eight

Allie rested her lunch tray against her hip, and checked the basketball courts, looking for Nathan. She spotted Cory, Mark, and the rest of their friends, but he wasn't there. Normally, she'd march off to the lab and drag him back to the sunshine and fresh air, but today she knew he was exactly where he needed to be.

Zoe saw her standing there and waved her over to their table under the big oak tree. Allie started walking toward them. But then she stopped. She pictured Nathan, alone in the lab, and wondered if he'd even stopped to grab lunch after fourth period. Knowing him, he hadn't. She held up a finger to Zoe, and then ditched the tray, gathered up her sandwich, chips, and her chocolate chip cookie, and started walking toward the lab instead.

Nathan was right where she expected he'd be, headphones on, fingers flying across his keyboard, eyes glued to his monitor. He didn't even notice her walk in.

She went straight to Ms. Slade's desk. "How long has he been here?"

"All through lunch yesterday. Well into last night. All through lunch today. I've tried to help, but he keeps saying he has all the help he needs."

Allie smiled to herself. Ms. Slade didn't know what that meant, but Allie did. He'd been chatting with Rachel, Kaiya, and Alexa ever since he left Allie's house on Tuesday night.

"I'm going to the teacher's lounge." Ms. Slade stood and gathered up her things. "I'll be back in ten minutes."

When she was gone, Allie walked to her workstation and sat down. She carefully ripped her ham and cheese sub down the middle and placed half on the desk between her keyboard and Nathan's.

He took his headphones off and draped them around the back of his neck. "What's this?"

"Crazy invention called food. Gives you energy. Keeps you sharp," she said, tapping her fingertip against her temple.

"Thanks." He reached for the sandwich and started unwrapping his half. Allie did the same with hers. He took a bite and washed it down with a big swig of water. "You shouldn't be here. You should be outside with all your friends. You're done."

"Finished."

"Whatever."

"I don't want to be outside with my friends. I want to be inside with you." She pointed at his monitor. "How's it going?"

Nathan shrugged. "It keeps glitching on this one part of the track, but Rachel had an idea this morning, so I tweaked the code a little bit and I'm hoping it will work. It passed the last test. I'm running one more to be sure." The two of them finished their sandwiches while they watched the progress bar move across the screen.

Allie ripped her bag of chips open and set them in front of him. "I usually give my chips to Emma—I'm not big on salty snacks—so you can have these, but I'm not giving you my whole cookie," Allie said as she unwrapped it and broke it in half.

"You can keep your cookie," he said.

"Nah, it's cool."

She handed it to him. As he reached for it, his fingers brushed hers. And then he looked up at her, and she met his eyes. He didn't move. Neither did Allie.

She thought back to those long days and late nights in the lab four months ago, when the two of them sat next to each other working on Click'd and Built, stuffing popcorn into their mouths, listening to music, working together to solve the problems with their apps that they weren't able to solve on their own. Somewhere along the way, while neither one of them had been paying attention, they'd gone from archenemies to friends. Allie looked down at their hands now, wondering if, this time, while they weren't paying attention, they'd gone from friends to something else entirely.

And then the door opened, and Ms. Slade breezed in, yelling, "Who wants popcorn?"

The two of them dropped their hands and the cookie fell to the floor. Allie giggled. Nathan chuckled under his breath.

"It's okay," Nathan said. "We didn't have any milk anyway."

Allie laughed even harder.

Ms. Slade set a bag of microwave popcorn down between them, just like she had countless times before. "How's it going over here?"

"Good," Nathan said.

"Fine," Allie said at the same time.

Ms. Slade patted them both on the shoulders. "Well, you're obviously busy here, so I'll leave you to it."

When she walked away, his computer let out a loud *beep*, telling him his game had passed the test. "I'm glad you're here. I wanted you to be the first to play it."

He picked up his phone and pressed a few buttons, and a second later, Allie's phone chirped with a new alert.

She launched his new game, and the familiar-looking neighborhood he'd created for Built came to life on her screen.

It looked a lot like his original—same streets, same houses, same billboards—but it was different somehow; larger, more animated-looking, not quite so detailed. The graphics were rounder, more colorful, and a lot friendlier. It was perfect.

The camera zoomed in close on two cars, a green one and a yellow one, waiting at the starting line.

"What color do you want to be?"

"Um. Yellow, of course," Allie said.

"Why yellow?"

"Because I'm fast as lightning."

She rested her elbows on her knees and held her phone in both hands, focusing on his game with everything she had. "I'm gonna win, you know?" Allie said without taking her eyes off the screen.

"No, you're not."

"Yes, I am. I'm great at racing games. Ask Courtney."

"I built this game," Nathan said. "I've been playing it for the last ten hours."

"So?"

"So, I know it backward and forward."

"Well, last time I checked, you were in the number one spot on my Swap'd leaderboard."

"What's your point?"

"If you can beat me at my own game, I can beat you at yours."

"Let's see you do it, Gator."

"Watch your screen, Nate."

A huge number three appeared on their phones. And then a two. Then a one. And then the word *GO!*

thirty-nine

"Allie! Dinner!" her dad yelled from the bottom of the stairs.

Bo raced out the door. Allie closed her laptop, slid off her bed, and followed him downstairs and into the kitchen.

Her dad was standing at the counter, spooning some cheesy-looking casserole thing onto a plate. Allie inhaled. It smelled delicious. Her stomach growled, and she realized she hadn't eaten anything since lunch.

Lunch.

In the lab.

With Nathan.

She pushed the thought from her mind for what seemed like the one hundredth time.

"Where's Mom?" she asked.

"She just called to say she was stuck in traffic and told us not to wait." He set a plateful of food in front of her. "How's everything going with Swap'd?" he asked.

Allie jabbed her fork into the casserole. "Better than expected," she said before she took a big bite.

She and Courtney had spent the last day creating a special version of Swap'd, and now Allie was putting on the finishing touches. It wasn't as interesting as the original, but it looked the same, and it gave her something to demo to the class the next day and something to show Naomi Ryan during her meet-and-greet at Game On. They had even put together a short video with pictures of all the CodeGirls who had helped her create it.

"It looks pretty slick," she continued. "It's a lot better than I expected."

"It sounds like you're feeling pretty good about it."

"I am." She was certain Ms. Slade and Naomi Ryan would both be impressed. And she was certain she was going to get an A on the assignment. She might even beat Nathan. Not that it really mattered to her anymore.

Her dad reached across the table and patted her hand. "You never cease to amaze me, you know. Then again, as your biggest fan, I might be a little biased."

"You think?" she asked sarcastically.

And then she heard the front door open. "I'm home!"

her mom yelled. Bo jumped up from his spot under Allie's feet and took off to greet her.

"This is going to be good." Her dad had a huge grin on his face.

"What are you talking about?" she asked.

"Turn around," he said, still beaming.

Allie looked over her shoulder.

Courtney was standing there with a duffel bag by her side.

Allie blinked hard. But when she opened her eyes, Courtney was still there.

She jumped from her chair, took three big strides, and threw her arms around her shoulders. "You're here!" She squeezed so hard, she lifted Courtney's feet off the floor.

"I'm here!"

Allie stepped backward and looked at her. "I can't believe you're here!"

"I can't believe it, either!"

"How long have you known?"

"Only, like, three hours! My mom surprised me. She picked me up from school and wouldn't tell me where we were going until we arrived at the airport. She even packed for me! She made me promise not to call you, but it was so hard not to! Our parents wanted it to be a surprise."

"Oh, it's definitely a surprise! The best surprise." Allie hugged her mom as hard as she could.

"We couldn't stand it," her mom said. "After all you two went through."

"As far as we're concerned, you two did exactly what we asked you to do," her dad said. "You figured out a way to get her here on your own."

"Thank you so much! I'll pay you back, I promise!" Allie said.

"You don't have to," her mom said. "We split the cost with Courtney's parents."

"You two can cover the next trip. This one's on us," her dad added. And then he changed the subject. "You must be starving. Sit. Let's eat and talk about what you want to do while you're here."

Courtney sat. "Allie keeps telling me how much fun it is to walk across the Golden Gate Bridge."

"That's easy." Allie's mom grabbed a notepad and a pen before she took her seat at the table. She started making a list. "The Game On conference is right downtown. The show floor opens at ten, and your meet-and-greet with Naomi Ryan is at eleven."

"And Nathan's presenting at the keynote at one o'clock," Allie added. "We don't want to miss that."

"Of course," her mom said. "You'll still have plenty of time to walk around afterward, and when you're finished, we'll head over to the bridge. What else?"

As the four of them ate, they planned the weekend. Coit Tower. Allie's favorite hot-chocolate place in North Beach. Lombard Street. Pier 39. By the time they finished dinner, they had a plan to fill every spare second until they had to take Courtney back to the airport on Sunday night.

Sunday. The thought made her sad, but she pushed it out of her mind. Allie couldn't think about the end when the two of them had a whole middle to look forward to.

Later that night, neither one of them could sleep. There was too much to talk about. Too much energy in the room. Too much adrenaline.

"Good day/bad day?" Courtney asked, staring up at the ceiling.

"You start," Allie said.

Courtney let out a sigh. "Bad day: I told my teacher about Swap'd."

Allie came up on one elbow. "You did?"

"Yeah. He told the principal and she made me shut it down. They didn't make me give everything back, but I had to give all the money to charity. And then, let's see, number two . . ." She thought about it. "It was harder to say goodbye to my mom than I expected. I miss her. And three, there was a lot of turbulence. How about you?"

"I'll start with good day . . . that's easy. One, you're here. Two, our Swap'd presentation is going to blow everyone away. And three . . ." Allie trailed off, thinking. And then she remembered what happened in the lab that day. She felt her whole face light up in the dark.

"There was this . . . thing that happened . . . with Nathan." As soon as she said the words, her heart started racing.

Courtney sat straight up. "I knew it!"

"Knew what?"

"You like him."

"No, I don't!" Allie sat up, too. "I mean . . . I don't know. I'm not sure. He's been my archenemy since third grade. We are constantly competing against each other. We're barely even friends!"

"Now I know that's not true."

"How?" Allie asked.

"You talk about Zoe, Maddie, and Emma *all* the time. You talk about Nathan just as often. But until last week, you never even mentioned Marcus to me."

"I'm sure I had."

Courtney ignored her and kept talking. "Think about it this way. How did you feel when Marcus told you he liked Zoe?"

Allie shrugged. "A little sad. Embarrassed. Lame for thinking he liked me that whole time."

Courtney nodded. "Now, how would you feel if Nathan told you he liked someone else?"

The thought alone made Allie feel like her heart had just shattered into a million pieces. She couldn't even imagine it. She would have been more than sad. She would have been hurt. And jealous. And kind of devastated.

"Oh my God," Allie whispered.

"See?" Courtney said. "Told ya."

friday

forty

"Next up, is Swap'd," Ms. Slade said as the giant screen at the front of the class lit up with the Swap'd logo. She stepped off to the side and Allie took her spot.

"Today, I'm going to tell you about Swap'd," Allie began. "I created it for this reuse assignment using code from three different developers, all friends I made during CodeGirls Camp last summer."

She clicked the remote and the slide advanced to a picture of Shonna next to an avatar that looked a lot like her.

"Shonna created an avatar builder for a game she made at camp. We took that and snapped it together with this auction game Kaiya made." She advanced the slide to a photo of Kaiya and a screenshot of her game, Going Once. "And then we added the calculation engine Jayne built. But most of the code came from this."

She advanced the slide again. "This was an app created by my friend Courtney called share|wear, which kept track of all the clothes we borrowed from one another during camp."

Allie gestured toward the back of the room. "Why don't you come up and join me, Courtney?"

Everyone in the class turned to look at her. Courtney covered her face and shook her head.

"Come on," Allie said. "I can't do this without you."

Courtney finally stood and joined her, and Allie advanced the slide again. "Here's where it all started."

On screen, Zoe appeared holding a pair of blue-and-gray earbuds out in front of her and wearing a dramatic pout on her face. Everyone in the class laughed. "My friend Zoe didn't get the wireless Beats she wanted for Christmas, so she bought these instead. And she was sad." Allie mimicked her pout, and everyone cracked up again.

Next slide.

"Zoe couldn't return them, so I had the idea to auction them off to the highest bidder during the bus ride home." In the picture, Zoe and Julia Sanders had their arms around each other. This time, Julia was holding the earbuds in her hands. They were both beaming.

Next slide.

Allie went on to explain how she and Courtney worked to pull everything together that night, reaching out to their fellow CodeGirls. "We couldn't believe how quickly it all happened. We tested it a few times over the next day, and cleaned things up a bit, and that was it. Swap'd was born."

Next slide.

"We held our first auction," Courtney said, pointing at the picture of the Swap'd interface on the screen. "And we made money."

"And then we held the second," Allie added, "and made even more money."

"We didn't make as much on the third one."

"And then we found out that selling stuff on campus is against our school rules . . ."

"And, also, the law."

The two of them talked fast, finishing each other's sentences.

"We can't actually sell anything, so today, we're going to hold a mock auction, just for the class," Courtney said.

They'd set it all up in advance, so with a push of a button, Allie sent Swap'd to everyone's phones. Within minutes, the whole class had downloaded and launched the game, and most of them were already creating avatars.

Allie and Courtney set the clock for one minute. Ms. Slade had given them six items to fake sell for fake cash. It was a fierce fight for Ms. Slade's bucket of Legos, and an even more vicious battle for all-you-can-eat popcorn.

When the auctions were complete, Ms. Slade returned to the front of the room and pretended to pass out the winnings, while Allie and Courtney wrapped up their demo.

"Thanks for swap'n'," they said at the same time. They high-fived each other, and the room erupted into applause.

"Excellent," Ms. Slade said when the cheers died down. "That is a perfect example of collaboration, code reuse, *and* being flexible." She made a wave motion with her hand. "Sometimes your initial idea doesn't work, but that doesn't mean you should quit on it. What else did you two learn from building Swap'd?"

Allie's hand shot up. "Check your idea with your teacher, just in case it's all illegal."

Everyone laughed.

"Yes, that's a solid takeaway," Ms. Slade said. "Okay, Nathan, you're up!"

He walked to the front of the room and launched his game. There was no logo. No fancy start-up screen. No over-the-top graphics. Just a simple yellow race car next to a green one.

"Forty-eight hours ago, I didn't have a game. I didn't even have an idea. And thanks to my friend Allie, I have this." He looked at her and gave her the biggest smile.

Under the desk, Courtney slapped her leg with the back of her hand.

"I've been having a hard time getting new users to try Built, so Allie had the idea to create a fun viral game that will draw new players in. I created this simple two-person racing game to introduce people to the Built world. I'll need two volunteers." Every hand went up. "How about . . . Xander and Kaitlyn." The two of them stood and walked to the front of the room, and Nathan handed each one of them one of Ms. Slade's demo phones, already loaded with his game and connected to the monitor. "You two ready?"

Xander nodded. Kaitlyn took a ready stance.

On screen, a huge number three appeared. Then a two. Then a one. And then the word *GO!*

Xander's little yellow car took off first, but Kaitlyn was right on his tail. Eventually, she caught up, and the two of them were side by side, until Xander pulled in front and cut her off, sending her into a tailspin. She recovered quickly, hit the gas, and started gaining on Xander again.

Everyone in the class was on their feet, screaming and clapping. Some people were cheering for Xander. Others were cheering for Kaitlyn. But Allie stayed silent. She wasn't rooting for one car or the other.

She was rooting for Nathan. She'd been rooting for him all along.

forty-one

The doorbell rang, and Bo went tearing off to see who it was.

"Pizza's here!" Allie's mom yelled, heading for the door.

"Finally!" Maddie said as she paced the kitchen. "I hate going from school straight to soccer practice. I'm always starving by the time we're done."

Allie's mom returned holding two large pizza boxes in the air over her head. "Make room for the good stuff," she said as she slid the boxes onto the counter.

"Oh, we've got room," Maddie said, rubbing her stomach.

Emma took a deep breath in. "That smells amazing."

Allie reached into the cabinet for the plates, and her dad grabbed a stack of napkins.

"Thank you, Mrs. Navarro." Zoe said, and the rest of them echoed her as they crowded in, preparing to dive forward and grab a slice as soon as Allie's mom was out of the way.

But Zoe spread her arms wide and turned around to face her friends. "Slow down. Guests first." Everyone took a step back. "After you, Courtney."

Courtney stepped into the newly vacant space and put two slices of pepperoni on her plate.

"You'll have to come back to visit in a few months, after the rain ends," Maddie said as she reached for a slice. "Then it's nice and sunny. Almost like the California they show you in the movies."

"I liked getting drenched during your soccer practice," Courtney said. "Trust me, I would have been disappointed if it looked like the California in the movies! I needed a weekend of rain."

"Who needs a weekend of rain?" Maddie asked.

"People who live in the desert," Courtney said matter-of-factly. Everyone laughed as they all gathered around the kitchen table.

"Tell us more about Phoenix," Emma said. "What are your friends like?"

"They're nice," Courtney said. "There's a big group of

us. Most of us were friends in elementary school, so we've known each other a long time, just like the four of you. But it's different, I guess."

"How?" Zoe asked.

"My friends are great, but they don't quite get my fascination with games and coding. Everything's fine on the volleyball court. We're all a team. But I'm kind of on my own with the other stuff I love. You've got one another's backs on the soccer field and off of it. Like the way you all stepped up to support Allie over the last two weeks—making slime, selling candy and clothes, divvying up all the cash, stuffing envelopes, and distributing it during lunch . . . That's pretty awesome."

Maddie, Emma, Zoe, and Allie exchanged glances.

"It was pretty great," Emma said. "We had Maddie spreading the word on KMMS."

"That was mostly to keep CrabbyPatty out of the scene," Maddie admitted. "Emma, that was all you with the money. You were a rock star." She looked at Courtney. "You should have seen her. She had a full assembly line going. She read the names, Zoe stuffed the cash in envelopes, and Chris and I delivered everything."

Emma looked proud. "Well, and we can't forget Zoe, the matchmaker," she said. "Thanks to her, Allie has an excuse to talk to Marcus for an hour a day, three times a week. No more of that *Hey, Six–Hey, Three* routine, right, Zoe?"

Zoe had a weird look on her face. "Right. So annoying."

Emma turned to Courtney. "Wait till you see Marcus. He is *a-dor-a-ble*. His hair is dark and kind of long, and it's always shiny—"

"He does have the *best* hair!" Maddie said. "But don't tell Chris I said that. He thinks *he* has the best hair at Mercer."

Everyone laughed.

"I loved meeting Nathan today," Courtney said. Allie looked at her wide-eyed, silently pleading with her not to say anything else. "Talk about cute! I've had a huge crush on his avatar alone, with those freckles across his nose and that spiky red hair." She wiggled her fingers over her head. "And now that I've met him in person . . ."

Allie felt her cheeks get hotter.

"I wouldn't be here if it weren't for him," Courtney continued. "He gave up his locker as the pickup point. And then he sold all that stuff on Swap'd when he could have sold it for twice as much anywhere else. Now *that's* adorable."

Maddie, Zoe, and Emma looked at each other. And then they looked at Allie.

"What?" Allie asked.

"Nothing," Maddie said. But she didn't look like it was nothing.

"Tell me more about Mercer," Courtney said, changing the subject. Maddie and Emma took turns telling her about their spot under the oak tree in the quad, and how they had to sneak their devices during the day or Mr. Mohr would confiscate them using his little orange bucket. While they talked, Zoe was unusually quiet, staring at the table and nibbling on her pizza crust.

When everyone else was distracted, Zoe leaned in close to Allie. "I have to tell you something."

Allie picked a piece of sausage off the pizza and popped it in her mouth. "I already know. And it's okay."

"It's okay?" Zoe asked. "Are you sure?"

"Positive." And then Allie whispered, *"¿Te gusta él?"*

"Do I like him?" Zoe's face lit up. "Yeah . . . I think I do."

"Good." Allie said it like she meant it. And she did.

saturday

forty-two

Allie and Courtney stood at the top of the escalator, looking down onto the show floor.

"Here we are," Allie said.

"I never thought I'd be here in a million years."

"Well, you won't be here in a million years. None of us will be."

Courtney rolled her eyes. "Cute. Come on. Let's go."

They followed the crowd into the exhibit hall and flashed their VIP badges for the security guard at the entrance.

Inside, it was loud and bright and big, and Allie couldn't figure out where to focus first. Enormous flat screens hung from the ceiling, all displaying the latest Spyglass games and trailers, and there were huge stages set up for demos and interviews with the development teams in all four corners of the room. Cosplayers walked the floor, and Allie and Courtney marveled at the fact that they could barely move five feet without someone stopping them for a picture.

"This is awesome," Courtney said. And then she repeated it about every ten minutes.

It wasn't too difficult to locate the Spyglass Games booth. It was smack in the middle and took up more space than any of the other ones. Right away, Allie spotted Jen, the one who helped her set up her kiosks during Games for Good.

She took Courtney by the arm. "Follow me. There's someone I want you to meet."

Jen was dressed like she was during G4G, in ripped jeans and black Converse, but this time, her hair was pulled back into a ponytail and she was wearing a black T-shirt with the Spyglass Games logo on the front.

As soon as she saw Allie, she stopped what she was doing and moved toward her. "Allie! It's so good to see you here!"

"Thanks for the passes."

"It was our pleasure."

"This is my friend Courtney," Allie said. "I told you about her in the e-mail I sent yesterday. We developed a new game together, so she's going to join me for the meet-and-greet, if that's okay."

"That's fine. Everyone's excited to see what you built,"

Jen said. "Hold on." She held one finger up and tapped the other one against her headset. "Okay, it sounds like she's on her way. Are you ready?"

Allie reached for Courtney's hand and squeezed it. "We're ready."

Naomi Ryan breezed into the booth and walked straight up to them. "Allie Navarro! I remember you." Allie wasn't sure if that was a good thing or a bad thing. She hoped it was a good thing. "It's so nice to see you again."

Allie stretched her arm out and gave her the firmest handshake she could. And then she introduced Courtney, and the two of them shook hands, too.

Naomi Ryan gestured to the two people with her. "This is Olivia Brannan and Jason Pierce. They're in charge of our summer hackathon program." They all did another round of handshakes. "I heard you both applied, so I asked them to join me. It sounds like you have something new to demo for us today."

"Yes, we do, Ms. Ryan."

"Please," she said. "Call me Naomi."

Allie tried to ignore her racing heart. She threw her shoulders back and straightened her spine, mustering up all the courage she could find. "It's called Swap'd. Courtney and I developed it together in about eighteen hours, using code from a bunch of our girlfriends who live all across the country."

"Really?" Naomi said. "I'm intrigued." Olivia and Jason nodded along.

Allie wasn't sure how many people would be there, so she'd borrowed three of Ms. Slade's demo phones and set them up in advance.

They'd already designed Naomi Ryan's avatar. It looked just like her, with short brown hair that flipped up a bit at the bottom, a red suit jacket that looked a lot like the one she was wearing the last time Allie had seen her, and a wizard hat, just for fun.

Naomi laughed when she saw it. "The hat is a nice touch!"

Allie handed Olivia and Jason two phones with generic avatars, and started explaining how the game worked.

They had already loaded six mock items into the queue: three of Courtney's favorite Spyglass video games, a pair of "SpyGlasses"—the new 3-D gaming goggles the company had announced the day before—a sweatshirt with the Spyglass Games logo, and a stack of Spyglass stickers.

"These items aren't actually for sale," Allie said. "So you can bid as high as you want. You have two minutes. Ready?"

Allie clicked the START button and the clock began counting down.

The executives were slow to start, so Courtney showed them how it was done, jumping right in with a $200 bid on the SpyGlasses. And that was all it took. Naomi put a $100 bid on the sweatshirt, a $30 bid on the stickers, and $100 on each of the games. Olivia and Jason were right on her heels, raising the bids.

"Get out of here," Olivia said to Jason when he raised the bid on one of the stickers to $4,000.

They all put money on the SpyGlasses, but then Courtney raised it to $5,000, outbidding everyone. "Oh, no you don't, Courtney. Those are all mine," Naomi said, increasing the bid on the SpyGlasses to $6,000. Courtney immediately raised it to $6,500.

The clock counted down. With thirty seconds to go, Allie and Jason were fighting for the sweatshirt, Olivia was taking a video game in a fairly uncontested race, and Courtney and Naomi Ryan were in a fierce battle for the SpyGlasses.

Naomi Ryan raised the bid to $10,000, but right at the last second, Courtney raised it to $10,001. Swap'd let out its congratulatory *cha-ching* sound.

"You got me!" She gave Courtney a high five. "Okay, this is fantastic!" she said to both of them. "How long did you say it took you to build this?"

"About eighteen hours," Allie said.

"And you collaborated with how many developers?" she asked.

"Three other girls, plus the two of us," Courtney said.

Naomi looked at Jason, and then at Olivia, as if the three of them were having a silent discussion.

"I think we're all in agreement about what we should do, aren't we?" she asked them.

"Absolutely," Olivia said.

"Total agreement," Jason said.

Naomi looked at Allie and Courtney. "Do you mind if I sell something?"

"Sure," Courtney said.

"Of course," Allie echoed.

Naomi Ryan typed quickly with her thumbs while the rest of them watched in silence. She pressed the START button and said, "Okay, check it out."

Allie and Courtney looked at their phones and read the description of the item she posted:

> Work as a mentor at Spyglass Games this summer! You'll be part of a small, exclusive team building the company's first teen-specific hackathon and mentoring participants! Candidates must demonstrate strong leadership skills, and the ability to work quickly and collaboratively. Three positions available.

Allie looked at Naomi Ryan. "A mentor? But we applied to be participants."

"Rather than participating in the program, we're inviting you to work closely with our in-house team to help build it. You'd be with us all summer, for eight weeks, and overseeing some of the weekend events. We think our hackathon program needs both of you. What do you think? Can you two handle a whole summer together?"

Allie's face lit up. Courtney's did the same.

"That depends," Courtney said. "Does your lab have gummy worms?"

Jason smiled. "All you can eat."

"Then we're in!" Courtney threw her arms around Allie, and the two of them jumped in place.

"We have one more mentor slot to fill," Olivia said. "Is there anyone you'd recommend?"

Courtney and Allie stopped jumping. They took a step back and smiled at each other.

"Are we thinking the same thing?" Allie asked.

"Yep," Courtney said. And then they turned to Olivia and, together, they uttered a single name.

forty-three

Allie knew Nathan's meet-and-greet was right after hers. She was hoping they'd pass each other so she could pull him aside and tell him what happened, but by the time she spotted him, he was already shaking hands with Naomi Ryan.

She and Courtney decided to walk the show floor and check out the other booths, but they were both in a bit of a daze.

"I think I'm dreaming," Courtney said.

"In that case, we're having the same dream. Maybe you should pinch me."

Courtney pinched her arm.

"Ow!" Allie jerked it away. "Not that hard."

The two of them spent the next hour stopping at booths, playing games, watching demos, and listening to presentations. Allie kept looking around for Nathan. She couldn't wait to hear about his meeting.

"I know what we need," Courtney said. "Follow me." She turned down an aisle, pointing at a demo station on the far side of the hall. And that's when Allie spotted Nathan walking right toward them, dodging a big group of people in cosplay. He waved at them.

Allie's mouth felt dry, her chest felt tight, and her heart was pounding. *Why was she so nervous?* She wasn't used to feeling like that around Nathan.

"Hey," he said. The three of them stood awkwardly in the middle of the aisle, people squeezing past them on either side. "How was it?"

"Amazing!" Allie said. "They loved Swap'd."

"I got in a war with Naomi Ryan over the SpyGlasses," Courtney said, puffing out her chest. "And I won. Of course."

"No way." Nathan's eyes grew wider. "You won a pair of SpyGlasses?"

"Well, it was a mock auction, so they were mock glasses. But I still won."

"How about you?" Allie asked. "How did she like your game?"

"She loved it," he said. "I have a meeting with the team next week to talk about how we can use it to draw new users to Built."

"That's great!"

"Yeah, it is." Nathan looked like he wanted to say something more, but he left it at that.

"Did you talk about anything else?" Courtney asked him.

Allie was glad Courtney had asked. She was dying to know.

"Yeah, they invited me to be a mentor at Hackathon." He shot Allie a sideways grin. "But you already know that, didn't you?"

Allie shrugged. "Not for sure."

"Naomi told me what you said. Right after I told her you were the one who gave me the idea for the racing game, and that you should get a spot in Hackathon."

"You recommended me?" Allie asked.

"Of course I did."

"And I recommended you."

Nathan nodded. "They all seemed to like the idea that we'd recommended each other. Olivia said it was a good sign that we'd work well together for an entire summer."

Allie shook her head slowly. "An *entire* summer with you? What was I thinking?" she joked.

"I have no idea."

It got quiet again. Allie didn't know what do with her

hands, so she shoved them into her back pockets. Nathan did the same with his. Neither one said anything.

"Well, Nathan," Courtney finally said, breaking the awkward silence. "The three of us will be spending the summer together. And since I'm Allie's friend, and you're Allie's friend, we should probably get to know each other better." She pointed at the booth at the far end of the aisle. "Like, I don't even know how you feel about zombies."

Nathan followed her gaze. "Oh, that's easy. I am one hundred percent anti-zombie."

"Hey. Me too!" Courtney's face brightened. "Are you any good at killing them?"

"Of course I am. You?"

"The best."

"Oh, are you, now?"

Allie felt like she was at a Ping-Pong tournament, watching the two of them go back and forth. "Uh-oh," she muttered.

"I'll take you on anytime," Courtney said.

"Now's good," Nathan said.

"Come on. We'll teach you, Allie."

"Oh, that's okay. I think I'll stick to racing games," Allie said, but it was too late. Courtney was already walking off, leading the way to a dark green booth with huge monitors and a sign that read BRAIN/FOOD.

Nathan hung back. "I like her," he said.

"I knew you would."

"Hey . . . I just wanted to say . . ." He rocked back on his heels and combed his fingers through his hair. "Thanks for everything, Gator."

Allie played with a loose string on her jeans. "Thank *you*, Nate."

For a moment, the whole convention center got quiet. The chaos around them—the bright lights, and the low hum of people chattering, and the loud music, and the people pushing past them—all faded into the background, and it was as if it was just the two of them working together in the lab. Helping each other. Competing with each other. Pushing each other to be better. Stuffing popcorn into their mouths. One-upping each other. Laughing at each other's jokes.

They were a good team. Everything about being with Nathan was easy. And fun. She no longer felt nervous or awkward or weird, because she had no reason to be. He was just . . . *Nate*. And now, he was standing there, smiling at her, face full of freckles, red hair all spiky and adorable looking.

Allie tried to play it cool. "Is there a zombie racing game anywhere? Because *that* I think I could do."

"Zombie racing?" he asked. "I don't think so."

"Well, maybe there should be. The zombies could race each other to the closest town, and whoever gets there fastest gets first pick at the humans."

"That's a little dark," Nathan said as they started walking toward the booth. "I love it."

"Yeah?"

"Told you. You always have the best ideas."

"Well you have all the racing code now. It would be easy. We start there. Snap on the leaderboard—"

"Use the avatar builder to make our zombies—" Nathan added.

"We'd need more cars," Allie said.

"And a lot more zombies."

"Want to build it together?"

"For what?"

Allie shrugged. "For fun."

"I'm in." He held out his hand and Allie shook it. Neither one of them let go right away.

"Helllloo!" Courtney was standing in front of a monitor, waving two game controllers in the air. Allie and Nathan dropped their hands. "I believe you have a game to lose, Nathan."

"You're going to eat those words," he said.

"No, I won't. I'll be too busy eating brains." Courtney handed him the controller. "Watch and learn, Allie."

The numbers appeared on the screen as the game counted down in green, gooey-looking font.

Allie stood behind them, watching the two of them play. It all felt surreal.

Courtney was there. Nathan was there. It was almost too perfect to be true. And then she looked around the room, taking in the lights and the sounds, enjoying the energy she felt in every corner of the room, feeling like she was exactly where she belonged.

acknowledgments

I have had the best time writing these Click'd books, and this one in particular. I think I typed the entire thing with a smile on my face, enjoying every second I got to spend with Allie and her friends.

The people in my publishing world are adults with kid-like hearts. Thank you to my editors, Emily Meehan and Hannah Allaman; copy editor Guy Cunningham; my marketing team, Dina Sherman, Holly Nagel, and Elke Villa; my publicists, Cassie McGinty and Seale Ballenger; and Mary Ann Naples, Sara Liebling, and Therese Ellis. Like many people, I *do* judge a book by its cover, and I'm especially grateful to designer Mary Claire Cruz and illustrator Jameela Wahlgren for creating covers that so perfectly (and adorably) capture the personalities of the characters you meet in the pages. Finally, thank you to my agent, Caryn Wiseman, for loving my tenacious girl coder when she was just an idea I had while on deadline for a totally different book. I kind of expected her to talk me out of writing Allie's stories and I'm so glad she didn't.

Okay, that's it for the grown-ups. Now I have a *bunch* of kids to thank.

My son and daughter are a constant source of creative inspiration. The initial idea for *Click'd* came from a conversation with my daughter, Lauren, and many of these moments in *Swap'd* came from brainstorming sessions with my son, Aidan. Thank you both for all you do to make my books better. Mostly, thanks for just being who you are and letting me look on with love and absolute awe.

I shamelessly steal many of my story ideas from my kids' friends, and they know it. Giant-bags-of-candy-size thanks to Alex Karp and Lanie Pritchard, whose entrepreneurial spirits are on full display in this story (details withheld to protect your secret ☺). Thanks to Maddie McCormick for that time you found your old DS and played *Mario Kart* for an hour-long ride in my car (I told you I was going to use that!). And thanks to Drew Frady, who will always be part of our family no matter how far away he lives. Here's to best friends who never let distance keep them apart for long.

I hold all the teen coders out there in such high regard. Thanks for inspiring others by example. Special thanks to Mercer Henderson for all she does to empower young women, but specifically for creating the brilliant closet-sharing app I borrowed here.

Thanks again to the friends who have been early readers, fact-checkers, and all-around great sounding boards on these books, including Ella Thorpe, Leslie Cary, and Hosanna Fuller.

Last but never least, thanks to all my young readers around the world. It is an absolute joy and the honor of a lifetime to write stories for you. Thank you for reading them, for sharing them with your friends, and for telling me when they speak to you. You make my job so much fun.